"Could be there's someone you already know who would make a fine daddy,"

Boone said to Chad.

Nixie touched his arm. "Boone, it's one thing to tease me, but please don't involve the children in your jokes."

"Who said I was joking?" Boone caught her gaze and smiled.

What could she do? Nixie looked at the man who had wedged himself so firmly into her life. The wispy blond hair that reminded her so much of her son's fell in disarray across his forehead. The smiling eyes were so incredibly blue. His face, like the man behind it, was strong, straight and full of character. And his lips, narrow and firm, tempted her with memories of their first kiss.

Did he truly think that something besides arguing and teasing could come of their relationship? Her eyes met his and she realized he was still waiting for her answer.

his gaze, immobilized ... headlights.

Dear Reader,

This month we have a wonderful lineup of books for you—romantic reading that's sure to take the chill out of these cool winter nights.

What happens when two precocious kids advertise for a new father—and a new husband—for their mom? The answer to that question and *much* more can be found in the delightful *Help Wanted: Daddy* by Carolyn Monroe. This next book in our FABULOUS FATHERS series is filled with love, laughter and larger-than-life hero Boone Shelton—a truly irresistible candidate for fatherhood.

We're also very pleased to present Diana Palmer's latest Romance, *King's Ransom*. A spirited heroine and a royal hero marry first and find love later in this exciting and passionate story. We know you won't want to miss it.

Don't forget to visit that charming midwestern town, Duncan, Oklahoma, in *A Wife Worth Waiting For*, the conclusion to Arlene James's THIS SIDE OF HEAVEN trilogy. Bolton Charles, who has appeared in earlier titles, finally meets his match in Clarice Revere. But can Bolton convince her that he's unlike the domineering men in her past?

Rounding out the list, Joan Smith's *Poor Little Rich Girl* is a breezy, romantic treat. And Kari Sutherland makes a welcome return with *Heartfire, Homefire*. We are also proud to present the debut of a brand-new author in Romance, Charlotte Moore with *Not the Marrying Kind*. When the notorious Beth Haggerty returns to her hometown, she succeeds in stirring up just as much gossip as always—and just as much longing in the heart of Deputy Sheriff Raymond Hawk.

In the months ahead, there are more wonderful romances coming your way by authors such as Annette Broadrick, Elizabeth August, Marie Ferrarella, Carla Cassidy and many more. Please write to us with your comments and suggestions. We take your opinions to heart.

Happy reading,

Anne Canadeo
Senior Editor

America's Publisher of Contemporary Romance

HELP WANTED: DADDY

Carolyn Monroe

Silhouette
R O M A N C E ™
Published by Silhouette Books
America's Publisher of Contemporary Romance

If you purchased this book without a cover you should be aware
that this book is stolen property. It was reported as "unsold and
destroyed" to the publisher, and neither the author nor the
publisher has received any payment for this "stripped book."

To Stephanie and Chad Greene
who, thank goodness, are better behaved
than my fictional children.

 SILHOUETTE BOOKS

ISBN 0-373-08970-8

HELP WANTED: DADDY

Copyright © 1993 by Carolyn Greene

All rights reserved. Except for use in any review, the reproduction
or utilization of this work in whole or in part in any form by any
electronic, mechanical or other means, now known or hereafter
invented, including xerography, photocopying and recording, or in
any information storage or retrieval system, is forbidden without
the written permission of the editorial office, Silhouette Books,
300 East 42nd Street, New York, NY 10017 U.S.A.

All characters in this book have no existence outside the imagination of
the author and have no relation whatsoever to anyone bearing the same
name or names. They are not even distantly inspired by any individual
known or unknown to the author, and all incidents are pure invention.

This edition published by arrangement with Harlequin Enterprises B.V.

® and TM are trademarks of Harlequin Enterprises B.V., used under
license. Trademarks indicated with ® are registered in the United States
Patent and Trademark Office, the Canadian Trade Marks Office and in
other countries.

Printed in U.S.A.

Books by Carolyn Monroe

Silhouette Romance

Kiss of Bliss #847
A Lovin' Spoonful #912
Help Wanted: Daddy #970

CAROLYN MONROE

lives within spitting distance of Flat Rock in Powhatan, Virginia, with her fire-fighter husband and two terrific children. Carolyn used to write feature articles for the local newspaper; she now prefers fiction to nonfiction because she can make up the facts. She has received awards for her writing, but better than that, she has received checks. Carolyn is a member of Romance Writers of America and the Virginia Romance Writers.

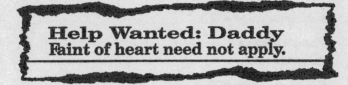

Help Wanted: Daddy
Faint of heart need not apply.

BOONE SHELTON
Lakewood, NC

Position Sought:
Father to Stephanie and Chad Thomas, and
husband to their mother, Nixie.

Education:
Graduate of the School of Hard Knocks.

Experience:
I've been a kid for thirty-three years, so I'd have
no trouble relating to Stephanie and Chad. As
Scout master and den leader, I've learned to give
children the kind of firm and loving attention I
wanted when I was young. In addition, I've had
lots of practice with love...I've been in love with
Nixie since I was nine years old.

*Special
Qualifications:*
I can lift four small children with one arm, teach
Chad any sport he wants to play, help Stephanie
laugh the blues away and show the kids how to
make fake boogers out of rubber cement.

Personal:
I'm a big man and, in my case, the old saying
"The bigger they are the harder they fall"
couldn't be more true. Nixie and her whole
family have stolen my heart...now all I want
is for them to take the rest of me.

Prologue

"Let me get this right. You two want to place a classified ad in my newspaper to get yourselves a father?"

The two children, Stephanie and Chad Thomas, looked up at Boone Shelton, disappointment evident in their eyes. He could tell they were afraid he was going to send them home before they accomplished what they had set out to do. He slowly rerolled his shirtsleeves and pondered the motive behind this unusual request.

The older child, a preteen girl, spoke up. "Actually, we're doing it for our mother. She can get dates...."

"Yeah, but once they find out about *us*," the boy piped in, hitching a thumb at his scrawny chest, "they don't come back."

The girl nudged her brother with her elbow. "It's not that we're bad," she hastened to reassure Boone. "It's just that Mom wants someone who wants us, too. And she wants someone *we'd* like. So this way we'd all be happy."

Boone leaned his bulk back in his chair and propped an elbow on a pile of papers stacked at the front of his desk. When the receptionist had brought the children back here, amusement twinkling in her eyes, and sat them in his office guest chairs, he'd seen their nervousness. To put them at ease, he'd moved his chair closer to theirs so the desk wouldn't be between them. Now he was beginning to wonder if he should have just sent them home and told them to stay out of trouble. But that wasn't his way. Besides, he was curious.

"So your mom sent you here to place an ad?"

"Oh, no!" the little girl replied. "We thought it up ourselves."

"Boy, will she be surprised when men start coming out of the woodwork!" the boy added.

The kids exchanged triumphant smiles.

Boone hated to burst their bubble, but he couldn't allow the types of men who'd be "coming out of the woodwork" to just show up on these nice kids' doorstep. Not only would their mother be displeased, but things could get unpleasant if some weirdo read the wrong message into their ad.

"Look, why don't you talk this over with your mother, and if she says it's okay, come back tomorrow," he said.

"Aw, man!" the boy said, punching his fist and scowling. "She'll just say no."

The girl extracted from her pocket a piece of paper folded to form a makeshift envelope. She opened it and took out a dollar bill and an assortment of coins. "We've been saving our allowance. We would have had more—" she narrowed her eyes at her brother "—but Chad bought a candy bar yesterday."

He seemed unconcerned by the accusation. "I'm a growing boy," he said innocently.

The girl got up and dumped the money into Boone's hands. "Is this enough to run the ad for three weeks?"

At a glance, he could see it was barely enough to cover the base rate for the first week. Somehow he couldn't bring himself to tell them that.

He studied the children more closely. They certainly were determined to go through with this. Their expressions reminded him of the P. F. Flyer incident of his youth.

After watching the black-and-white television commercials, he'd been convinced that owning a pair of P. F. Flyer sneakers would enable him to run so fast he'd take off and fly, just like the kid on TV.

His mother could have simply told him it was nonsense to think a pair of sneakers would make him fly. Instead she'd let him find out for himself. He'd bugged the neighbors for odd jobs and earned the money for the prized sneakers. When he'd insisted on having a "test flight" in his new shoes, his mother had sought to soften his crash landing by piling old blankets at the end of the board takeoff ramp he'd rigged up in the backyard.

Not only had she cushioned his behind, but she'd cushioned his pride and taught him a valuable lesson, as well.

"Well," she'd said casually as he'd rubbed his sore backside, "looks like we can't believe everything we see on TV." In his young mind, he'd thought she was every bit as surprised by the disappointing results as he was.

And now these kids thought an ad would bring them all they'd ever wanted. He didn't have the heart to tell them it would bring more of the same kind of men their mother had already met, or that it might be ignored altogether. Most likely the latter. And in a weekly paper in a town the size of Lakewood, North Carolina, the ad would create more curiosity than tangible results.

Boone thought once again of those P. F. Flyers.

"Since you're first-time advertisers with the *Lakewood Crier,*" he said, returning half the money they'd given him, "you're entitled to the first-timer's discount. There's just one catch."

Both children looked up, suspicion darkening their brown eyes.

"It has to be a blind ad. That means any, uh, *applicants* will write to you in care of this paper. They won't know who you are unless your mother chooses to contact them."

The girl let out her breath. "Good. That way, we can weed out the perverts."

"Well, yeah, to put it bluntly," Boone said.

She blushed. "Sorry. I didn't mean to embarrass you."

Boone grinned. These kids were something else. "So, what do you want the ad to say?"

The sister cleared her throat. "'Help Wanted: Father. Strong, loving, dependable. Prefer someone as good-looking and smart as our mother.' Oh, and don't forget, 'Must like kids and animals.'"

They'd obviously rehearsed it well. Boone finished jotting it down and turned to Chad. "Is that okay with you, son?"

"Yeah, but change it to 'Help Wanted: Daddy.'" When his sister shot him a stern look, he explained, "A father is someone who goes to work, reads the newspaper, and punishes you when you're bad. But a daddy is someone who plays ball with you and lets you work on the car with him. That's what I want...a daddy."

Chapter One

After the kids missed their school bus, Boone offered them a ride to Mrs. Thomas's place of business nearby. But first, he made them call her to get permission to ride with him.

He'd been a little surprised that she hadn't asked to speak with him and had given her okay after only a moment's hesitation. When he met her, he planned to take her aside and tell her she should be more careful about who she let those terrific kids ride with.

As he drove, the children chattered excitedly about how many and what kind of people might answer their advertisement.

As they pulled into the parking lot at Cordaire Signs, Boone felt his stomach do its familiar flip-flop at the mere sight of the name.

Nixie Cordaire. The girl who'd grown up two houses away from him. The pretty, petite girl who'd captured his heart and tied his tongue. The problem was, in his adolescent awkwardness, he'd shown his affection by teasing her mercilessly.

Boone hadn't had a chance to look her up since he'd returned home to Lakewood after buying the *Crier* a couple of months ago. He wondered if there was a man in her life. Probably. He couldn't imagine anyone would overlook a gem as precious as Nixie Cordaire.

He hoped she was out of the office. When they did meet again, he wanted to be prepared so he'd say just the right things. It was when he had felt off-balance and unprepared that he'd tormented her with relentless teasing.

"Thanks for the ride, Mr. Shelton." The kids climbed out of the car and torpedoed into the small building where their mother worked. He followed them in.

Boone followed their voices to the back office and found the kids talking excitedly with...*her*.

He didn't know how it was possible, but she was even more beautiful now than she'd been in high school. She was still petite—still had that same delicate bone structure and graceful way of moving that made him think of a ballerina. Her auburn hair was longer, though, and styled so it emphasized her heart-shaped face...from wide-set, golden brown eyes to a pointed chin that begged him to cup it in his hand.

She looked up at him and watched him warily as if waiting for him to make the first move.

"Little Nixie Cordaire," he said softly.

Nixie narrowed her eyes. Even after all these years, he was still treating her as if she were his kid sister. "I've grown up." *In case you haven't noticed,* she added mentally. "And my name's Thomas now."

Boone's eyebrows drew together. "Thomas Cordaire?"

Nixie sighed and fidgeted with her small gold earring. He was doing it again—deliberately goading her. It seemed some things never changed.

"Nixie Thomas," she said with forced patience.

"So you're divorced." He couldn't imagine any man being foolish enough to let her get away.

"Widowed."

"I'm sorry." The instant he said it, Boone knew it was a lie. He only hoped the guy had deserved her.

"Mom, we decided to find us a daddy," Chad blurted.

"And we're going to find you a husband," Stephanie added.

Nixie's startled gaze shot to Boone, then back to the kids. "You did *what?*"

Boone couldn't help himself. The years-old habit hit him as strongly as it had when they were children themselves.

"Oh, come on, Nixie. You don't need to pretend you knew nothing about your kids placing a personals ad for you."

As her eyes widened and her mouth formed a small O, Boone plunged recklessly ahead.

"If you'd like, I could go through my phone book and fix you up with someone nice."

"Really?" said Stephanie and Chad in unison.

"Of course not," Nixie snapped. Then her tone softened. "He was just kidding."

She looked askance at Boone as if to double-check that he *had* been joking.

"Why don't you two tell me what you were doing at the newspaper office?"

After they gave their scrambled version of what had transpired, and Boone had offered his two cents' worth, Nixie turned to him, one hand on her jeans-clad hip.

"Boone! How could you?" She tossed her hair with one hand, as she'd always done when perturbed with him. "It's one thing to involve me in your corny teasing, but to drag two little kids into your silly prank..."

"I'm not little," Chad insisted. He pushed up his sleeve and flexed his wiry arm to display a puny muscle. "See."

Boone picked the boy up and tucked him under one arm as casually as a businessman carries a newspaper. Chad giggled at the unexpected action.

"It's not what you think," said Boone.

"How could you allow—even encourage—the children to proceed with such an ad?"

"Sometimes," Boone began, "it's best to let kids find out for themselves that P. F. Flyers won't make you fly."

"What?"

Even Stephanie, who was doodling on a pad of paper at her mother's desk, stopped and waited for his explanation.

"What I'm trying to say is that if I hadn't let them place the ad they would've been disappointed and it would've squelched their initiative."

By now, Chad, still dangling under Boone's arm, was moving his arms and legs in a slow swimming motion. "Aw, c'mon, Mom. Be a sport."

Nixie rolled her eyes. She could tell it would be impossible to make Boone see how foolish such a scheme was.

"It's a blind ad," Boone assured her, "so no one will know it's you. Besides, there probably won't be many responses."

The kids were waiting expectantly for her answer. She worried that they might be disappointed when their plan failed. But they would be disappointed if she said no after all their effort. Still, Nixie wasn't happy about being pushed into a corner.

Finally, reluctantly, she agreed to let them pursue this crazy plan.

"All *right*," said Chad from his airborne position.

Stephanie beamed.

Boone smiled. "It might be fun. And who knows, you may find the man of your dreams."

Nixie had a sickening feeling that the man of her nightmares held her love life in his brawny hands.

Boone tugged at the frilly pink dress that had ridden up around his waist. Under his stiff khaki pants, the panty hose bagged around his knees and ankles. He resisted the urge to pull them up.

Across the road at the elementary school, Cub Scouts and their parents gathered at the front door, waiting for someone to unlock it. He hated being late, especially when Scouts were depending on him. And even more so, when he'd talked Nixie into bringing Chad to watch the Cub Scout rehearsal tonight. Maybe the kid would enjoy the camaraderie enough to join the pack.

Boone patted his overcoat pocket to check for the key and sprinted across the road.

Too late, he saw the blue sedan round the corner without stopping. With the skill of a lifelong athlete, he leapt to avoid a direct impact. His body glanced off the front fender, then connected solidly with the hard pavement. His world went black.

Talk about being in the right place at the right time, Nixie thought. She had stopped at the squad building to check the training schedule before heading home. That was when the call came about a hit-and-run accident.

Another volunteer arrived while she was pulling on her jumpsuit.

This time the victim was lucky. Jeff pulled the ambulance up at the accident site just four minutes after they received the call. Nixie hoped this kind of luck would hold out until they could recruit and train more volunteers.

Jumping lightly down from the cab of the ambulance, she grabbed her bag and trotted back to where a dozen little boys in blue uniforms and neckerchiefs gathered around a man in an overcoat.

"Excuse me, coming through."

Kneeling beside the unconscious form, she checked his pulse and respiration. Both were steady and strong.

Nixie's breath caught in her throat as she realized the blond-haired giant she tended was none other than Boone Shelton. Briefly she wondered if this was another elaborate setup for a joke at her expense. Fortunately her paranoia left as quickly as it came. Boone would never joke about something this serious.

She took another look at his massive body lying so still on the pavement, and it scared her. She'd never seen him so helpless and vulnerable before. Boone had always been the protector, never the protected.

Nixie became aware of Jeff moving the crowd back, and she turned her attention to the lump on Boone's forehead. She had to stay busy—partly to help Boone and partly to keep from reacting emotionally to the fact that the boy she'd grown up with was lying helpless before her and needed her more now than he ever had.

He appeared to have some slight road rash on his hands and across his cheek, but the lump—and his unconsciousness—was what concerned her most. She pushed the shaggy blond hair off his forehead to closer examine the injury.

Boone winced and his eyelashes fluttered before they opened and he focused on Nixie. "Well," he murmured, "if it isn't little Nixie Cordaire. Still taking care of people, aren't you?"

Nixie let out a big breath she hadn't realized she'd been holding. "Boone? What are you doing here?" she asked for lack of anything better to say.

Boone cautiously glanced around him. "Lying in the middle of the road, presently."

Jeff knelt beside her. "How is he? Should I call for the chopper?"

"No, I don't think that'll be necessary. Why don't you get the gurney while I check for fractures?" Turning to Boone, she said, "Let me know if it hurts."

"You'll be the second to know."

Aware of those pale blue eyes watching her every move, Nixie felt almost shy as she ran her hands over his neck, shoulders, arms and legs. *Just pretend he's the dummy you worked on in training class,* she told herself. But there was no way she could mistake his overdeveloped frame for that of the training dummy. Moving her hands to his abdomen, she pressed lightly to check for obvious internal injuries. He showed no sign of pain.

"If you're finished poking me," Boone said, attempting to rise, "those Cub Scouts are waiting for me. Ohhh." He pressed a hand to his head and leaned back on one elbow.

"Don't try to get up. You took quite a whack to your forehead. You ought to let a doctor look at that."

"What about the dress rehearsal?" one of the mothers asked.

Boone fished a key out of his coat pocket and tossed it to the woman. "Go on without me. I'll be back in an hour."

Nixie gave a delicate snort. "When's the last time you've been to an emergency room?"

It was a good thing Boone had regained consciousness because Nixie doubted she and Jeff and all of the Cub Scouts together could have lifted him into the ambulance. Well over six feet tall, the massive physique that had been easy to distinguish on the high school football field was now even broader than it had been fifteen years ago.

"What do you weigh these days, 230?" she asked after he lay down in the back of the ambulance.

"No, I'm kinda puny now. Down to 218."

"Puny" was hardly the word to describe Boone Shelton. His chest seemed big enough to land an airplane on, and his arms bulged against the sleeves of his overcoat. Odd, but why would he be wearing an overcoat on such a balmy spring day as this? She adjusted the straps that secured him to the gurney and signaled Jeff to begin the drive to the hospital.

"This is a first for me," said Boone.

"Riding in an ambulance?"

"Being tied to the bed by a beautiful woman."

There had once been a day when his teasing would have reduced her to blushing and stammering. Fifteen years, one marriage and two kids later, she didn't blush so easily. But she would have stammered if she hadn't clamped down on the inside of her bottom lip.

"No blushing? What happened to the pink cheeks Nixie Cordaire was always famous for?"

Nixie squirmed on the padded bench beside him. Why was it that, even though he was reclining, he seemed to tower over her? Nixie busied herself by inspecting his forehead.

She hadn't changed much since high school, thought Boone. Whenever her composure was rattled, she turned her attention full force to whatever job was at hand. And she was doing it again. He ought to know. He'd rattled her composure often enough in his day.

Boone felt the moisture bead up on his temple and trickle back into his hairline. How could a person stand to wear so many layers?

"You must be burning up in that overcoat. Let me help you."

Before he could stop her, Nixie unfastened the top button.

Boone's big hands closed around hers. More than anything, it was shock that stilled her helping fingers.

Pink ruffles and white lace spilled from the vee of his coat. Dusty blond chest hairs sprang from the frilly neckline. She'd seen stranger sights during her years as a volunteer rescue worker, but never had she been more surprised than now.

Dragging her eyes away from the froufrou, she met Boone's gaze. "Blue is more your color," she said, immensely pleased to have caught him with his pants down, so to speak.

If she didn't know better, she would have sworn Boone Shelton reddened. "I was on my way to a dress rehearsal for the Cub Scout play. Remember?"

Nixie gave up all hope of keeping the humor out of her expression. She raised one eyebrow.

"I play the part of . . . Dorothy," he said.

This was too much.

"Right," she retorted, "and all those Cub Scouts are munchkins."

Of course she believed him. Nixie felt certain that anyone with Boone's reputation with the ladies wouldn't be inclined to dress in women's clothing. Besides, she knew he would have better taste than to wear that awful polyester thing for kicks.

After all those years of putting up with his endless teasing, she could finally get even. She couldn't pass up an opportunity as good as this.

"Listen, I know a couple of really nice guys. Maybe we could, like, double-date sometime."

"Yeah, yeah, really funny."

"Come over to my place, and I'll show you how to shave your legs."

The ambulance pulled to a stop. While Nixie unbuckled her seat belt, Boone refastened the top button of his coat.

Nixie released the gurney for Jeff, and Boone fumbled with the restraints that held him down. "I can walk."

Once inside, Nixie and Jeff persuaded him to sit in the wheelchair and pushed him to the ER nurse.

"Got a live one this evening, Virginia." Nixie winked at the head nurse. "This is 'Dorothy,' who *claims* he was on his way to a dress rehearsal play."

The woman quickly sized him up and boomed, "Hello, Dorothy! What seems to be your problem?"

Boone shot Nixie a look of grudging admiration for zinging him with the kind of teasing he'd dished out to her over the years.

Since the emergency room was unusually slow tonight, Boone was processed, examined and x-rayed fairly quickly.

Nixie told Jeff to take the ambulance back to the station. Then she called Uncle Jim to ask him to bring over one of his shirts. He assured her that Aunt Laura would give the children supper, and tried to ferret out the reason for the shirt.

"It's for a friend," Nixie responded, hoping he wouldn't ask too many questions. Lying wasn't one of her strong points, and even though she'd taken delight in serving Boone his own brand of teasing, she didn't wish to get her uncle involved in the joke. "He was in an accident," she added, hoping Uncle Jim would deduce that Boone's shirt had been bloodied or torn.

By the time her uncle arrived, Boone was ready to be released. Fortunately, he didn't have a concussion—just a goose egg over his left eyebrow. After a brief reintroduction to Jim, he gratefully accepted the shirt and pulled it on.

Nixie couldn't help appreciating the way his thick arms stretched against the short sleeves. Although buttons strained across the chest, the fabric was lax over his trim abdomen.

Her perusal was abruptly interrupted when Virginia called out, "Hey, Dorothy, don't forget your dress." She held up a large paper bag.

Uncle Jim's eyebrows shot up when Boone went back to retrieve the bag. "Dorothy?"

"Uh, let me carry that for you, Boone."

Uncle Jim followed Nixie to the nurse's desk. He eyed the bag she'd practically yanked from Boone's hand. "A *dress?*"

"Uncle Jim, please don't start."

"Oh, don't worry about him," Virginia reassured with a wave of her hand. "I'm sure his toes point the right way in a bathroom stall. He was wearing men's boxers under his panty hose."

Boone grinned, and it seemed as though he were enjoying the notoriety. In the waiting room, an elderly woman pursed her lips and glared at him.

"You've changed a lot since we last saw you," her uncle said. Then he started to laugh, his ample stomach bouncing in rhythm to his hearty chuckles.

Boone laid a hand on the older man's shoulder as he and Nixie followed him out to the car. "And you haven't, Mr. Cordaire."

"... And after Uncle Jim learned about the dress, he was like a pit bull with a meaty bone. He wouldn't let go," Nixie told her aunt. "He offered to stop at the pharmacy on the way to Boone's house so he could pick up some cosmetics and panty hose. Then Uncle Jim asked whether he preferred to wear front- or back-hook bras." Nixie took a handful of popcorn, then passed the bowl to her daughter. "Boone was a good sport and dished it right back, but I was beginning to feel uncomfortable for him."

"So you still have feelings for him." Aunt Laura's statement was more of an observation than a question.

Nixie shook her head. Her aunt and uncle had been like second parents to her since her father's job had taken him and her mother away from the east coast just months before Paul died.

In his own irrepressible way, Uncle Jim had sought to lighten her spirits with teasing and practical jokes. In the process, his infectious humor had shaped eight-year-old Chad into a relentless prankster who frequently made eleven-year-old Stephanie the victim of his mischief.

Aunt Laura, on the other hand, had provided a calm and steadying influence for Nixie and the children. In the past eight years, since Paul's death, hers had been the shoulders Nixie cried upon and leaned on. As well as being a pillar of strength for Nixie, Aunt Laura was also the unwanted matchmaker in her life. Nixie considered the possibility that her aunt was now pointing a Cupid's arrow at her high school nemesis.

"The only feeling I ever had for Boone Shelton was dread of being in the same room with him. He couldn't stand me, and he let me know it by constantly picking on me."

Laura bestowed a loving smile on her husband, who had assumed his regular Friday night position in the wide recliner where he watched rented movies. Stephanie and Chad, perched on the padded chair arms, cuddled against their great-uncle and ate popcorn out of the bowl balanced on his stomach. "Your Uncle Jim used to pull my hair. That's how I knew he was interested in me."

Jim looked up from the TV and grunted his disagreement. "Your hair looked too thick and pretty to be real. I was just checking to see if it was a wig."

The children giggled.

"Even if that was why he picked on me, which I doubt," said Nixie, "it wouldn't work. Boone's not my type."

"Why not?" asked Stephanie, who was starting to take an interest in the opposite sex.

"Because," Nixie said, trying vainly to put into words why she was opposed to a relationship with Boone. For lack of a better explanation, she said, "He's a jock."

"So?"

"So she's saying," Uncle Jim piped in, "she'd rather have a couch potato like me."

"What kind of man are you looking for?" Aunt Laura prodded.

Nixie thought a moment and gave a little sigh before answering. "I want a man who reads and can carry on a discussion about a good book. My wish list is for someone who's intelligent and sensitive to other people's needs. And, of course, someone who would be a good father for Stephanie and Chad."

Aunt Laura patted Nixie's arm. "Honey, you're not going to find another Paul. You ought to widen your horizons a little. Besides, that very well could describe Boone Shelton. He has a lot going for him, and he's a successful businessman, what with being the new owner of the *Lakewood Crier*."

"Anyone can buy and manage a small newspaper." She wondered if the paper was all that had brought him back to his hometown. In a moment of peevishness, Nixie doubted he'd last more than six months with the dying publication that had earned the nickname "Lakewood Liar."

Aunt Laura peered through the top of her bifocals at Nixie. "Just as anyone can buy and manage a sign shop?"

Her aunt had ever-so-gently put her in her place. Paul had helped her buy the shop—now known as Cordaire Signs. Although it had been a healthy business when she'd bought it, it had nevertheless been a trial, not only to learn the system but to make the business grow. It had been a mental and physical challenge to make Cordaire Signs run like a well-oiled machine.

"Touché," she conceded.

"Mom," Stephanie whined, "Chad said he left Tarzan's cage open so the bird could chase my cat."

Chad smiled as if proud that he'd managed to goad his sister yet again. To make matters worse, Uncle Jim was doing a poor job of hiding his amusement at the sibling squabble.

The movie was over and it was time to go home, anyway. "Come on, let's go see if Tarzan is terrorizing the cat."

Nixie hugged her aunt and uncle good night while Stephanie sprinted across the lawn to their house next door.

When they entered the spacious trilevel home, everything seemed to be in order. She soon located a safe and purring Precious. Knowing the parrot's favorite pastime, Nixie checked the venetian blind cords to see if Tarzan was swinging on them. No sign of the feathered trapeze artist anywhere.

She found Chad in front of the cage that held its own special place in the living room. He was grinning devilishly. "I must've made a mistake," he said. "Tarzan's all locked up, nice and tight."

"Mom, he knew it all along. You've got to do something about that little . . ." Stephanie ranted on with a tirade of complaints about her little brother.

Nixie tuned out her daughter, but continued thinking about what Stephanie had said. She would have to do something about Chad's antics. His pranks were coming more frequently. None had been malicious, but they did seem to be growing in severity.

Her uncle's encouragement hadn't helped matters. Nixie recalled with a shudder the time she'd found the fake vomit in her shoe. Chad had borrowed the prop from Uncle Jim's "gag bag." Yes, she definitely had to do something about her son. But what? She suspected that what he needed was a man's firm hand. A man other than Uncle Jim, that was.

Remembering her aunt's matchmaking comments, Nixie knew she'd need a better reason than Chad's discipline to get involved with a man.

Chapter Two

Nixie was stripping bedsheets and the children were performing their Saturday morning chores when the doorbell rang.

"Close the door—Tarzan's loose," Chad shouted as she opened it to find Boone Shelton on her front porch. Wearing a teal Henley shirt with the sleeves cut out and jeans that were sliced at the knees and frayed on the thighs, he looked like the most scrumptious vagabond she'd ever seen. She was glad to notice the lump on his forehead was almost gone and only a pink scrape remained.

"The scarf's a nice touch," he said, referring to the bandanna that secured her hair.

Suddenly self-conscious, Nixie touched a hand to her head. Why was it that his mere presence made her feel like an insecure teenager again?

Remembering the parrot, Nixie grabbed Boone's elbow and urged him into the foyer.

"I didn't realize you'd be so glad to see me." He glanced pointedly at his elbow, where her hand still rested.

Hurriedly slamming the door shut behind him, she said, "The bird is out."

"I beg your pardon?"

At that, a raucous jungle yell reverberated from the living room. Boone gave a startled expression and took a step back.

"Oh, that's just Tarzan," she explained. "He's swinging on his vine."

Boone stared at the woman who was even more beautiful now than she had been at sixteen. That was the last time he'd seen her before going off to college and to make his mark in the publishing world.

"Won't you come in?" Nixie led him to the living room, where Chad dusted the television set, Stephanie picked up newspapers and stacked them in a bin, a yellow cat cowered under the couch, and a green and red bird dangled at the end of a venetian blind cord, its wings flapping almost in rhythm to a popular tune blaring from the radio.

"Hi," said Stephanie. "Welcome to our zoo."

Chad dropped his dust rag. "Did anybody answer our ad?"

Nixie shot them both a quelling look. Boone grabbed the boy and pretended to punch him in the stomach. "Not yet, sport. The ad only came out today."

He let go of the laughing boy and turned to Nixie.

"I didn't mean to interrupt your chores. I stopped next door to return your uncle's shirt." Boone withdrew three tickets from his pocket and handed them to Nixie. "And to bring you these. They're tickets to the Cub Scout play tonight. Your aunt and uncle said they'd be there." He watched the wariness skitter across her delicate features. "I hope you can come, too."

"Are you going to wear that pink dress Uncle Jim told us about?" asked Chad.

Boone rumpled the boy's blond hair. "Sure, and if you want, you can try it on after the play."

"No way, José."

"Boone, if this is payment for our rescue and taxi services yesterday, a donation to the squad would be more beneficial."

He hadn't intended the tickets as payment for her help. He'd merely wanted her seated in the audience. He wanted her to be his good luck charm again.

Every time the dark-haired lovely had accompanied his sister to the school football games, Lakewood High had taken the trophy. Boone remembered scanning the crowd for her face and playing his best after he'd found her. If only he'd been able to tell her how much her presence had meant to him. Or how much it had hurt when she'd brought a date.

But, even if he'd been able to express his feelings, she wouldn't have given him a second glance—for Phoenix Cordaire had been pretty and popular. She was known for being a giver and spent much of her spare time tutoring others, visiting at the nursing home, and helping organize the annual local walkathon for spina bifida.

Boone, on the other hand, was known as "Boone the Goon," the jock who was involved in every sport from football to wrestling. He'd been convinced she'd never look twice at him. Maybe his relentless teasing had been a subconscious effort to push her away before she had the chance to reject him.

"I'll send a check next week, but I still want you to come tonight." She hesitated, so he decided to play dirty.

"I'm sure Stephanie and Chad would like to see it, especially since they missed the rehearsal last night. Wouldn't you, kids?"

"Say yes, Mom. It sounds like fun," Stephanie pleaded.

Chad was more direct. "Yeah—I want to see Mr. Shelton dressed like a sissy."

A buzzer blared in another room. Nixie seized the opportunity to leave the room and collect her thoughts before answering. She wasn't sure she was ready for the feelings that surfaced whenever she was around him. "Excuse me a minute," she said as she headed for the stairs. "My washing machine's off-balance."

Stephanie waited until her mother had left the room and directed a meaningful look at her brother. "That's not the only thing around here that's off-balance."

Boone sat down on the couch and was startled when the forgotten parrot demanded behind him, "Did you brush your teeth?"

Preparing to scold the bird, Chad shook his finger at it. Tarzan beat him to the punch and yelled, "Shut up, stupid!"

The boy seemed surprised, but he quickly covered his embarrassment by admonishing, "You're supposed to be on my side."

The bird flew across the room and landed on top of the wall clock. "Cuckoo," said Tarzan.

Stephanie giggled and told the bird, "I'm sure Mr. Shelton knows that already."

Boone laughed out loud, and the parrot followed with a giggle that sounded remarkably like Stephanie's.

"How old are you?" Boone asked her. He was amazed that, even though her hair was honey-colored instead of auburn, she looked so much like her mother.

Chad answered for his sister. "Mom said she's eleven, going on forty."

"Hmm," said Boone. "That's even older than me." He liked the kids, probably because their spirit reminded him of Nixie. Despite their contrary comments, he could tell they really liked each other. Maybe he could recruit the boy into his Scout pack. With a lot of rationalizing, he could even convince himself that his motives for doing so were purely altruistic.

He listened patiently while Chad described a martial arts technique he'd seen on a television cartoon.

Downstairs in the utility room, Nixie deliberately dawdled with the laundry while her kids raked this latest male visitor over the coals. They weren't bad children, but their high-spirited antics had been known to chase away more than one gentleman guest. She considered them her human litmus test. She'd even cross-stitched a pillow that indicated her opinion on the matter. Love Me, Love My Kids.

Nixie had restarted the washer and was going up the steps when she heard Chad yell, "Hii-iii-yah!"

Immediately after, Boone's voice rang out and Nixie heard a loud thump. Uncertain what her son had done this time, she ran to the living room.

Boone lay flat on his back, and Chad's eyes were wide with excitement. "I flipped him, Mom. All by myself!"

Stephanie rolled her eyes. "Chad, you're such a dork sometimes. Couldn't you tell he *let* you do it?"

Boone grinned, the action reminding Nixie of the many times he'd looked at her in just that way before delivering a verbal gibe.

"Are you all right?" she asked.

He rose from the floor and stood in front of her in a fluid motion not normally expected from a man with his bulk. "I'm fine. We were just horsing around."

"Mom doesn't let us horse around in the living room," Stephanie announced.

His eyes never leaving Nixie's, he asked, "Does she allow it in the bedroom?"

"Sometimes," said Chad, "if we don't play too rough."

He grinned at Nixie. "Oh, I don't believe in playing too rough in the bedroom, either."

Nixie swallowed. She wasn't sure whether it was the way he pinned her with his gaze or the double entendre of his words, but either way she was feeling quite warm. She had always been the loser in their verbal wrestling matches; she dared not speculate about a bedroom wrestling match. Regardless of the outcome, the idea didn't seem totally objectionable.

"Be ready at six-thirty," he said, moving toward the door.

She was ready now.

"I want us to get there early so Chad can watch the backstage goings-on before the play."

Nixie abruptly came back to reality and followed him outside. He flashed her a smile and jogged across her yard on the footworn path between her house and her aunt's and uncle's, where his car was parked. Nixie couldn't help admiring how the shirt emphasized the broadness of his back or the way those tattered jeans clung like a second skin to his muscular buns and thighs.

He was in his car and gone before she remembered she hadn't agreed to attend the play.

* * *

Tonight was bingo night at the squad building. It was also Nixie's turn to call the numbers, but another volunteer agreed to fill in for her.

While the kids bickered about whose turn it was to clear the table, Nixie concentrated on making herself look perfect. Whenever she was feeling less than composed inwardly, she took extra pains with her outward appearance to help bolster her confidence.

She kept the jewelry simple so she wouldn't look out of place at the gathering of Cub Scouts and their families. The tulip-shaped yellow and black dress accentuated the curve of her waist and hips, stopping at a flattering level just above the knee. She wished she had more curve for the top part of the dress but quickly rejected the urge to fill that area by other means. Even so, she'd achieved the effect she wanted. Being flawless on the outside helped cover a multitude of cracks in the armor underneath.

When Boone arrived at the Thomas home for the second time that day, he was presented with a sight so breathtaking all he could do was stare. Gone were the jeans, sweatshirt and scarf. She was the girl of his dreams, only much more grown-up. He let his eyes drink in the sight of her, committing the picture to memory.

He wanted to tell her how stunning she looked—how the light floral scent of her perfume taunted him, making him want to kiss her until those doelike golden brown eyes closed from the pleasure of it. But he didn't know how to put those impressions into words. Instead he reverted to his past behavior and changed the subject. "Are Chad and Stephanie ready?"

Nixie blinked. She'd been caught up in the intensity of his gaze, immobilized like a deer dazzled by headlights.

Then, abruptly, his words had brought her out of the spell as surely as if he'd snapped his fingers. Perhaps she had imagined the strange force that had seemed to pass between them. As Stephanie would say, she needed to take a reality check.

At the elementary school, the reality was that Boone Shelton was quite popular with the children. The young boys flocked around him, begging to see how many he could lift with one arm. With three of the smaller children dangling from his flexed limb and two clinging to his back, he caught Nixie's eye and grinned. "It's one way to keep fit."

Nixie smiled back. Most men who'd been as large as Boone had been in his teens would have become soft and overweight by their thirties. But not Boone. He put too much stock in his body to let it lose its tone. Nixie remembered the exuberance with which he had thrown himself into high school sports. With his superior build and single-minded determination, he became the star of every athletic event he entered.

As the boys' excitement level rose, so did their volume. Boone easily brought them under control with a quiet admonishment and set each to a particular task. Nixie was pleased at how smoothly he involved Chad with the rest of the boys and solicited Stephanie's help in arranging the props onstage. No child was favored over another, but each was made to feel special.

Even Nixie was made to feel useful, handing out photocopies of the typewritten script and coaching the youngsters on their lines. She was engrossed in helping one forgetful youngster when a wave of giggles swept through the classroom where they had assembled.

Looking up, she saw Boone in that notorious pink dress. With a neck like a tree stump, broad shoulders, hairy arms, narrow hips, and thick legs, he looked anything but sissy.

The tacky red wig that sat askew on his head seemed incongruous with the hard, chiseled lines of his face and faint shadow of beard on his jaw. The stuffing in the front of the dress had migrated to form two asymmetric lumps. And the white panty hose he had put on—and managed to run—clearly defined the flattened curls of leg hair that liberally covered his shins and calves. Large-size sneakers finished the ensemble.

"Look," exclaimed Chad, "it's Boone Hilda!"

The room exploded with good-natured laughter.

A scowl grew on Boone's face. It was a look that could make a street gang member tremble in his shoes. Walking slowly and deliberately to Chad, he clasped the boy under each arm, lifted him to eye level, and gave him a stern glare.

The room grew deadly silent, and all eyes turned to stare at the pack leader and the new kid. Chad's expression was a mixture of confusion, fear and curiosity.

Stephanie timidly tugged the lace ruffle at Boone's elbow. "He didn't mean it, Mr. Shelton. He was just kidding."

Nixie opened her mouth to demand that he put her son down, but he spoke first, his voice deep and menacing.

"The name is Dorothy," he growled at the boy. "Dorothy Priscilla Lillywhite." For emphasis, he gave Chad a gentle shake. "And *don't* you forget it!"

Chad's face split into a broad smile. The rest of the boys gathered around the pink giant, clamoring, "Scare me, Boone, scare me."

Nixie slowly let out her breath. From the time she was seven—when the Sheltons moved to Lakewood—until she was sixteen and Boone moved away from home, she had never seen or heard of him using his size to bully or intimidate anyone.

She knew he'd never harm or even frighten anyone intentionally. Nixie chalked up her reaction to a mother's protective instincts.

"Did you see that, Mom?" Chad's face was flush with excitement. "He almost scared the pudding out of me!"

"Me, too." That was at least partly true.

Boone disengaged himself from the tangle of boys who swarmed around him like gnats. He crossed to where Nixie stood with her family and, after play-boxing with Chad, draped his arms around the shoulders of both Stephanie and Nixie.

"It's almost time for the show to start. I've reserved front-row seats for you ladies—and your aunt and uncle." Lightly tugging Stephanie's hair, he added, "I expect you to lead the applause for us."

Stephanie blushed under his flirting wink, reminding Nixie of the many occasions on which he'd made her blush and then teased her about her pink cheeks. "What about Chad?" Stephanie asked.

"If he'd like, he can help out backstage and watch the play from there."

Judging from her son's reaction, she would have thought he'd been invited by the president to have dinner at the White House. She gave her consent after making him promise not to touch anything unless specifically instructed. Boone flashed her a questioning glance but remained silent.

Uncle Jim and Aunt Laura waited for them in the front row. The play was much more entertaining than Nixie had anticipated. From missed cues to forgotten lines to dropped props, the boys happily fumbled their way through their parts. They actually seemed to enjoy the hysterical laughter coming from the audience. Occasionally, Nixie and her family could see Chad, offstage, helping a boy change costumes or handing another his prop.

"Look, Mom," whispered Stephanie, "Chad's not playing tricks on anyone."

Nixie crossed her fingers and, satisfied that her son would behave himself, focused her attention on Boone. Although his entrance had been met with swells of laughter, he seemed perfectly at ease playing the part of a young girl who had moved to a new neighborhood and was shunned by the previously all-boy residents.

Despite his comical appearance, Boone played the part with great sensitivity. He was so convincing that the Scout who was Dorothy's main tormentor actually apologized for being so mean. Action stopped for a moment while Boone whispered instructions to the boy who soon picked up in the script where he'd left off.

Nixie was amazed that, no matter who forgot a part, Boone was able to prompt the child with the correct line. He must have memorized the entire script!

The play ended shortly after Boone, still acting the part of Dorothy, came onstage with a BMX bike and performed a series of awesome stunts. Even in a dress, his was an incredible body to watch.

For their parts, the Cub Scouts didn't have to act out their amazement at Boone's performance—the emotion was genuine. Nine mouths gaped open in unison.

When Nixie realized her expression matched the boys', she snapped her jaw shut. A familiar feeling swept over her, and she recognized it as the same one she'd felt every time Boone had scored a touchdown or pinned a wrestling opponent to the mat. Back then, she'd considered her possessive pride in his achievements to be related to her connection with him via his sister. Since she and Ellen had been close, Nixie had been happy for him in his accomplishments, just as she would for a brother . . . sort of.

The play ended with the boys making friends with the girl, and Dorothy offering to teach them some of her stunts.

As the curtains closed, Nixie was left with a warm, comfortable glow deep inside. She attributed the feeling to the production's happy ending.

"Wasn't he terrific?" said Aunt Laura.

"Yes," Nixie agreed. "I couldn't get over how well he played his part."

"Played his part? I was talking about what a terrific job Chad did handing the actors their props and closing the curtains at the right time."

Nixie faltered. Of course Aunt Laura had been talking about Chad's ability to concentrate on his assignment and do a good job of it. Nixie had been so enthralled with Boone that she'd forgotten to look at her own son.

Aunt Laura watched her with undisguised speculation. Embarrassed by her faux pas, Nixie groped under the seat for her purse. Finding it, she stood and led her family backstage before Aunt Laura started with any probing questions.

The hall leading backstage was crowded with parents and well-wishers. After the crowd thinned and they congratulated Chad on his role as stagehand, Boone broke away from another group and came over to join them.

"Weren't these boys great?"

"They were wonderful." Nixie couldn't help adding, "And you were very believable as Dorothy."

He'd changed out of his costume, but easily slipped back into his role. He slanted a saucy grin at Nixie. "A girl does what a girl has to do."

Nixie decided that he was one of the most unique men she'd ever known. So secure was he in his own masculinity, he was comfortable donning a dress for the Cub Scout play and even joking about it. She felt certain that should someone try to goad him about his part, he would refuse to take offense.

Come to think of it, he'd been much the same way in high school. Despite the energy and enthusiasm he had poured into sports, he hadn't seemed to care what others thought of his athletic accomplishments. If he had fumbled a ball and was chided about it, he'd shrug and say, "I missed. So what?" He had been equally blasé about praise he'd received for pushing his team to victory. Whereas the attention might have unsettled other boys during those traumatic teen years, Boone had seemed unaffected by it all.

One fringe benefit of being the star player was that he never lacked for a date with a pretty girl. He was even low-key about that. More than one of Nixie's friends who had been interested in him—but too shy to let him know it—remarked how lucky she was to see him almost every day. *Right,* Nixie had thought at the time, *I'm so lucky to have him torture me every time I visit his sister.*

An hour later, after the Scouts had cleaned the school auditorium and her aunt and uncle had taken Nixie's children home, Boone locked the school door and led her to his car in the rear parking lot. The car, like its owner, was big yet understated. The vehicle was a quality machine, but not flashy.

The night was cool. There were no clouds to hold the day's warmth close to the earth. Stars glimmered brightly,

competing with the moon for top billing, and the blink-
ing lights of an aircraft passed high overhead.

Boone slowly walked past the sole car in the parking lot
toward the fence that enclosed the football field. He
seemed remote, as if in a trance.

Nixie walked up behind him. Her eyes followed his to
the muddy playing field. She remembered the times he
had played in conditions such as this. No matter how
many layers of mud he'd worn, she'd never had any difficulty spotting him. And no matter how ruthlessly he'd
teased her—even on the day of the game—she'd always
cheered him on from the stands.

Boone broke the silence. "Sure brings back memories."

From the tone of voice, Nixie knew that even though
he'd pretended only a mild interest in the game, it had
meant much more. It had been as if much more than
winning or losing a game had been riding on how well he
played.

He opened the gate and waited for her to step through.
They walked together in silence. When they reached the
bleachers, Nixie sat primly on the lowest bench and
hugged her arms.

He was used to seeing her near the top row, giggling
with his sister. Her movements, though more refined with
practice and the confidence that came from growing
older, were the same, however. *Yes, indeed,* he thought,
it sure brought back memories.

Boone jerked his thoughts back to the present. If he
didn't keep his mind on target, he'd forget the reason he'd
asked to speak to her tonight. Quickly, before his mind
wandered back to the way her hair shone in the moon-
light, he described Chad's interest in joining the Scouts

and the benefits of membership. He was surprised when she resisted the suggestion.

After all Scouting had done for him—helping him grow from the shy, awkward new kid in the community to someone confident in his own abilities—he couldn't imagine anyone turning down the opportunity for her child to join...unless, of course, she had problems getting him to the weekly den meetings.

"If transportation is a problem, I'll be glad to give him a ride."

Nixie paused before answering. She wondered how to explain the protectiveness she felt toward her son—her baby. Unless someone had been through what she had with Chad, she doubted he would understand the tight bonds she felt for him. Uncle Jim had called those bonds apron strings, but she couldn't bear to think of anything bad happening to her child after all he'd been through already.

"The transportation isn't a problem. I just...don't think it's safe to let him do some of the risky activities that are required."

"*Risky* activities?"

Nixie stiffened, preparing to be ridiculed yet again for her protectiveness. Or, as Uncle Jim called it, "overprotectiveness." "Yes. I consider camping, woodworking, rough sports—that kind of thing—too risky for Chad."

She was glad she couldn't discern his expression, for she was sure he thought her silly, just as everyone else did.

Instead of ridiculing her, however, he started describing the activities and ways in which the leaders safeguarded against injury. She could see he wouldn't let up until he had convinced her Chad would be safe in his care...or until she explained why she still couldn't take the chance.

"Chad was born after a difficult delivery. The doctor didn't think he was going to make it, but the little rascal pulled through, anyway." Even now, it still amazed her that he'd ever made it through those first few days. "Just when we thought the crisis was over, he stopped breathing in his sleep. The first few times, Paul was there to help me revive him. Then after Paul died, it was up to me to go to Chad every time the monitor alarm went off. I guess you could say he has 'died' a half dozen times already."

Nixie fought to still the trembling that had little to do with the evening's chill. "As a rescue volunteer, I've seen enough victims to know that no activity is completely safe. I couldn't forgive myself if either of my children were involved in a preventable accident."

After a moment of silence, Boone asked, "Could you forgive yourself for depriving your children of opportunities to grow?" He wouldn't push too hard, but he couldn't give up, either. "Let him come to the den meeting Wednesday after school. The most strenuous activities they'll do is memorize pledges and make crafts from the handbook. Give him a chance to focus that energy of his on something that interests him. You might even find he'll be less inclined to harass his sister if he has something else to occupy his mind."

At that, Nixie's temper exploded. How dare he imply that her son's mischief-making was related to her protectiveness? "Tell me...how many children have *you* parented?"

He didn't seem the least put off by her defensiveness, which only irritated Nixie more.

"Not counting the Scouts, none. But not for a lack of wanting."

She peered at him through the darkness. She could tell that, this time, he wasn't teasing.

Somehow this latest revelation didn't rest well with Nixie. It was as though an object she'd always seen as round suddenly turned out to be triangular.

If he'd claimed to be a womanizer or even an Olympic contender, she'd have had no trouble dealing with that information. She'd never seen him as domestic material, perhaps because his competitiveness made him seem like an unsuitable candidate for the give-and-take of a family situation.

"What's the matter?" he asked. "Don't you think Boone the Goon would qualify as a family man?"

Chapter Three

Nixie's eyes jerked up to meet his. "I never thought of you in that way. It was a horrible nickname, and I don't know why you used to let people call you that," she said with more vehemence than she'd intended.

He shot her a skeptical glance but said nothing.

Nixie wasn't sure why, but it bothered her to think he doubted her sincerity.

The first drop of rain hit Nixie's cheek and trickled down to her chin. In a few more seconds, she and Boone were running across the sodden field, back to the car. Doors opened and slammed shut, and bodies dripped water onto the leather upholstery.

Laughing and winded, Nixie said, "We could have walked and gotten no wetter than we are now."

"Ah," Boone corrected with a finger held aloft. "But then you wouldn't be breathing hard and fogging the windows."

Nixie cut her eyes at him. It was as if time had stood still for fifteen years. Only Ellen was not here to tell her brother to shut up.

"Could we call a truce for the next, say, thirty or forty years?"

Boone put a hand to his chin as if considering her suggestion. "If you want to call a truce, it must mean we're at war and you're losing. If you're losing, that means I get to seize all your property. Personally, I think that sounds like more fun than a truce."

He was not going to do it again. Nixie was not going to let him make her blush or stammer or react in any of those embarrassing ways she did as a kid.

"Look, nobody's going to seize anyone else's property." She tried not to focus on the mental image that accompanied her words. "The only thing I want from you is your promise not to encourage Stephanie and Chad in this 'daddy' ad or any future such brainstorms."

He stretched back against the seat and draped his right arm behind her. "I don't want to see them get hurt any more than you do. But," he reminded her, "they did spend their own money for the ad."

"I realize that, but I'm just asking you not to get them overexcited about this cornball idea." In a gesture of annoyance, she swept her hair away from her face and flipped the ends over her shoulder. The damp tendrils fell limply across Boone's arm.

"We're both soaked to the skin. Let's go dry off, and then we'll talk about this some more."

He drove only a block and a half and pulled in at the centuries-old tavern that housed the *Lakewood Crier*. Inside, he led her past the empty receptionist's desk, which was complete with computer, offices that were occupied by even more desktop publishing systems and laser printers, and a room with a large slant-top table and assorted clip-art books and large paste-up sheets. The modern inside of the building provided a sharp contrast to the historic exterior.

Boone opened a wooden crossbar door and led her up a narrow staircase to a small apartment. With a minimum of furnishings other than body-building equipment and an absence of curtains, it looked like a man's apartment. A Cro-Magnon man's apartment.

Nixie smiled. "How quaint."

"It's not much to look at yet, but it has everything I need—" he pointed into the cramped kitchen "—including a dryer." Without preamble, he peeled off his shirt and tossed it into the machine.

Nixie's eyes were drawn to the broad, firm planes of his chest and abdomen. Liberally covered with golden brown hair, his torso was so wide she wondered if her arms could encompass it. She wondered whether it was curiosity or the strange sensation in the pit of her being that made her want to try. The upper part of his arms seemed as big around as her thigh.

Her gaze fell to the purplish mark that began on his left hip and disappeared beneath the waistband of his trousers. A hematoma that size would last at least another week before it faded completely. From his casual stance, he appeared not to be aware of the dark bruise or her reaction to it. Yes, indeed, this was a Cro-Magnon's apartment, and here was the resident Cro-Magnon.

"I swear I won't jump your bones. There's even a lock on the bedroom door if you don't trust me."

Nixie jerked her attention away from his hip to the amused expression he wore on his face. "What?"

"I said, give me your dress and I'll throw it in the dryer with my shirt. Come on, I'll get you a robe to wear." He led her down the short hall to his bedroom and rummaged in the drawer for a terry-cloth robe, which he tossed to her. Then he got out a black T-shirt and pulled it on. Nixie had been relieved to see him covering his bare chest, but the sight of him in that tight shirt was just as distracting.

He left the room and was pulling the door shut when he leaned back in with a grin. "Let me know if you need anything else."

When the door finally clicked shut, Nixie took a big breath to calm her frazzled nerves. "What you *need* is a swift kick for what you're thinking," she muttered to herself. "He didn't ask what you *want*." As a widowed mother of two, she knew she would be wise to forget about those particular wants. At least for now.

Doffing the wet dress, she let it fall to the floor and shrugged on Boone's enormous robe. On him, it was probably knee-length. On her, it fell to the middle of her calves. She wrapped the front flaps tightly about her and knotted the belt around her middle. Even though she still wore her half-slip and camisole, she felt naked underneath the robe.

She was glad, when she emerged from his bedroom, that he made no teasing comments about her appearance. Instead he took her dress to the kitchen and returned a moment later with two cups of hot coffee.

Aside from the television and a bench press, the only piece of furniture in the living room was a brown plaid demisofa. She sat down and, with a little squeezing, he joined her. Although it was made to seat two people, Nixie was sure it hadn't been designed with Boone in mind.

He had turned at an angle to face her. Having crossed one ankle over the other knee, his thigh hovered disconcertingly over her lap. Trying to ignore his proximity, she tried once more to elicit his support in discouraging the children from their wild-haired scheme.

"Look, about that ad..."

He looked up and gave her his full attention. It was all Nixie could do to keep from drowning in the ocean-blue depths of his eyes.

"It would make things a lot simpler if any replies were, well, discreetly disposed of." She was acting in the children's best interest, so why did she feel like such a heel for making this simple request?

"This is the kids' ad," Boone said gently. "They're entitled to all the replies that come from it."

Nixie fumed. It was impossible to argue with someone who wielded logic as his weapon. "What about dangerous or crazy people? Surely you know that they're the only kind of people who would answer such an ad."

Boone chuckled. "Does a person have to be dangerous or crazy to look for love or a place in a family?"

"You're ignoring my point," Nixie persisted. "I don't want my kids reading angry or foul letters from someone with an ax to grind."

"You're right."

Nixie breathed a sigh of relief that he was finally beginning to see reason.

"You're their mother," he continued, "and it's certainly within your rights to take away from them whatever you think might be harmful."

The rat! He wasn't giving in after all. He was going to force her into the role of bad guy by making her take away the letters he brought to her children.

Boone set his empty cup on the floor and leaned back, clasping his fingers behind his neck. The thought entered Nixie's head that with this posture he created a bigger target for a thrown object.

Opting for a more prudent alternative, she followed suit and placed her cup on the floor. She stood. "Obviously, you aren't willing to see reason, so I may as well quit wasting our time."

"Suit yourself," said Boone, making no apology for his inflexibility. "I'll get your dress."

He came back a moment later, clutching a yellow and black garment that looked as though it would fit a large doll.

"What did you do to my dress? It was almost new!"

Boone at least had the grace to look sheepish. "If I were you, I'd take it back. This sucker shrunk to half its original size."

"Give me that." It was just like Boone Shelton to heap insult on top of injury. It was bad enough having her simple request refused so callously, but now this. She shook out the dress and held it against her. The bottom barely cleared her hips. "There's no way I can wear this home."

Her glare warned him not to make one of his typical smart-alecky replies.

The ride to Nixie's house was filled with a tense silence. Boone broke the standoff as he pulled into her driveway.

"I'm sorry about your dress. It looks like I owe you a new one."

"You owe me, all right." She got out before he could come around to open the door. She was furious with him—but not about the dress. That could be easily replaced. Even so, she wanted him to pay...for the dress, for insisting on giving letters to her children after she'd asked him not to, for implying she wasn't doing a good job of raising her son. Most of all, she wanted him to pay for those years of merciless teasing. "Yes, sir," she said. "You owe me for a lot more than this dress. You can start paying me back by forgetting that my kids ever placed that crazy ad in your paper."

"I'm sorry." He took a step closer, as if his very nearness would soften his answer. "I can't do wrong by your kids just because you asked me to... even if you are a friend."

"Friend?" How could he have ever considered them such? They'd been at each other's throats all through school, and it looked as though the cycle was starting all over. "If you treat your friends like this, I'm glad I'm not your enemy."

Her voice rose along with her temper. With trembling fingers, she untied the terry-cloth sash at her waist and yanked off the bulky robe. "Here," she said, thrusting the garment into his arms. "Don't ever let it be said I accepted any favors from you."

With a haughty whirl, she turned away from him and stormed toward the house. To Boone, in the twilight her white lingerie made her look like a tiny spirit floating across the lawn.

And like a spirit, she was just as hard to pin down. When the apparition disappeared into the house without so much as a glance over her shoulder, Boone got into his car and drove off.

He wouldn't be able to wear that robe again without thinking of her.

Nixie stomped into the house and slammed the door behind her. Unmindful of her appearance, she walked into the living room, where her aunt and uncle looked up from their television show.

"Well," said Uncle Jim, "it looks like you had a nice time."

Tarzan eyed her from his cage and let out a jungle yell.

"You—" Not in the mood for the bird's shenanigans, Nixie pointed a finger at the parrot.

"Shut up, stupid!" Tarzan finished for her.

"Sh-hh!" If he kept up like that, he was sure to wake the children.

"Nixie, don't argue with the bird." Aunt Laura got up to cover the cage. "You know he always gets the last word."

With the feathered commentator quieted, Aunt Laura turned back to Nixie. "Are you all right? Did Boone hurt you?"

Nixie shifted the dress to her other hand and crumpled it. "I'm fine. My dress was ruined in his dryer after we got drenched in a downpour."

Uncle Jim grunted his annoyance. "I lent him my shirt. I don't see why he couldn't have done the same for you."

"He lent me his robe, but I gave it back." At their questioning glances, she stretched and faked a yawn. "I didn't mean to stay out so late. Thanks for putting the kids to bed."

"Anytime, dear." Aunt Laura kissed her cheek.

Nixie could tell there were questions her relatives wanted to ask. She was glad they didn't voice them, because she certainly didn't have any answers. As she closed the door behind them, she decided life would be much simpler if she could avoid Boone Shelton altogether.

Over the next week and a half, she tried many times to put him out of her mind, but frequently found her thoughts returning to him.

One morning, as she was reading the *Lakewood Crier,* she couldn't help noticing the new image the twice-weekly paper sported lately...more professional and much less biased than when Mr. Yoden had owned the business. Even many of the advertisers who had, over the years, taken their business elsewhere now returned with large, eye-catching displays. One of the new features was an advice column. And, along with the changes in format and content, the name had been changed to the *Lakewood Gazette.* She supposed that was Boone's attempt to stop the Lakewood Liar jokes.

Yes, indeed, he was a man of honor, and the business owners of Lakewood knew it. It was just too bad he couldn't—or wouldn't—relax his honor where her kids were concerned. She supposed she should be glad he was so steadfast about doing the right thing, but she wished he could also foresee the problems it could cause.

Regardless of Boone's code of ethics, she couldn't just stand by and watch her kids get hurt—or worse, scared—when they read the letters that might come from their ad.

Níxie had ignored her children's squabbles about who should get the prize from the cereal box. Now, however, she looked up to find Chad with his finger poised and ready to flick a piece of cereal at his sister. She gave him a quelling glare, and he reluctantly popped the tidbit into his mouth.

Boone might be the rough-and-ready type, but her children weren't. They still needed protection, and she was determined to provide it for them. She would just have to be extra diligent with Boone to make sure they were protected from his good intentions.

When Boone showed up unexpectedly the next evening, she didn't let him rattle her composure.

"I didn't know they made Cub Scout uniforms that big," she said, referring to his khaki shirt and pants.

"Mom, he's the den leader," Chad pointed out.

Boone, however, refused to be goaded. "The bigger the kid," he replied, "the bigger the uniform." Turning his attention to Chad, he added, "I'll bet you can get one in your size, too."

"Can I, Mom?"

She fixed a warning glare on Boone, but he appeared not to notice it. He was certainly the most hardheaded person she'd ever met.

"He missed last week's den meeting," said Boone. "There's plenty of room in my car, so there's no need for him to miss this week, too."

Nixie pushed her hair behind her shoulders with a defiant flip of her wrist. "We've already talked about this."

"We also talked about depriving children of opportunities to grow." To Chad, he said, "What have you achieved in your spare time since I saw you at the play?"

The boy grinned proudly. "I taught Tarzan to bark at Stephanie's cat."

Boone opened his hands in a resigned gesture. "I rest my case."

Stephanie obviously overheard and came in from another room. "Mom, you've *got* to do something about that kid."

Nixie sighed. She supposed Boone had been telling the truth when he said the most strenuous den meeting activities would be memorizing pledges and making crafts. Maybe she could at least let Chad try it. "He hasn't had supper."

"I'll buy him a burger."

"Friend for life, man!" Chad and Boone exchanged high-fives.

Chad dashed out to the car, then stopped to see what was holding up the den leader. Boone had been a little slower to leave. Lingering on the porch, he acted as though he wanted to say something else to Nixie. When Chad called out to him, he winked at Nixie and said, "See you in a couple of hours."

His words sounded more like a promise than an idle comment. With a peculiar sense of anticipation, Nixie found herself looking forward to seeing him later that evening.

She watched as Boone and Chad drove away. One large blond man and one small blond boy. To the uninformed, the two could pass for father and son.

Less than two hours had gone by when Nixie started worrying. She wasn't used to Chad going away with anyone other than Jim or Laura. They should have had time to eat a hamburger, attend the hour-long meeting, and return by now. She paced the living room again and pulled the curtain back to peek out. Maybe she shouldn't have let him go after all.

"Chill out, Mom," said Stephanie. "He'll be back soon. You ought to enjoy the peace and quiet while you can."

A little more than two hours passed before she heard car doors slam, followed by excited male voices.

Chad entered, carrying a large department store bag. Boone smiled in a self-satisfied way. It was enough to make Nixie wonder what mischief they'd been up to.

Boone nudged the boy. "Show her what you got."

That was all the prompting Chad needed. In seconds, the floor was scattered with official Cub Scout uniform parts, including cap, neckerchief and patches.

"Where did you get all this?" Nixie asked, puzzled by the unexpected purchase.

Boone cleared his throat. "After the meeting, I figured we weren't too far from the mall, so we saved you a trip."

The mall was at least five miles out of their way, but before Nixie could point this out, Chad declared, "I'm a real Scout now, Mom. Next time, I won't be the only one wearing play clothes."

"Who said anything about next time? I thought you were just going to try it out and see if you liked it." Turning to Boone with one hand on her hip, she waited for an explanation.

"He did try it out, and he liked it. Since we got the uniform tonight, you'll have time to sew the patches on before the next meeting."

He seemed quite pleased with his forethought, but Nixie wished he hadn't taken it upon himself to do this. She felt pushed into a corner.

"You really shouldn't have done it," she said, sweeping a hand to indicate the items Chad was admiring, piece by piece.

Boone sat on the couch. "It was the least I could do after what happened to your dress. I would have bought you a replacement, but I don't know your size."

"Don't worry about it. In my job, I don't wear anything fancier than jeans and T-shirts."

Chad interrupted by jostling Boone's knee. "Don't forget to give this to Stephanie."

Boone took the small white box from the boy and handed it to Stephanie. "We saw this in the store and thought of you."

Nixie watched as her daughter tentatively opened the box and lifted out a pair of miniature satin ballet slippers on a pink velvet rope. "Thank you," she whispered. Gingerly, she draped the necklace over her head. "This is beautiful. Whose idea was it?"

In unison, Chad and Boone pointed at each other.

"I'm going to go look at it in my mirror," she said, and ran upstairs.

"I'm going to try on my new uniform." Chad disappeared up the stairs behind his sister.

The room seemed suddenly silent without the children's chatter. Even the parrot was quiet for a change.

Nixie settled into the chair beside Boone and tucked her feet under her. "Don't you know Santa's not supposed to return for another nine months?"

"I like your kids. They're good people."

Nixie looked at him suspiciously. She thought he had been joking, but one look at the sincere smile on his handsome face told her he meant what he said. Hadn't he seen by now what little stinkers her children could be?

The few other men who'd come to her home had chosen not to return after the first visit. She had suspected they'd been put off by the mere presence of the children, and here was a man who claimed to like them even though they could be very rambunctious at times.

She turned her attention to him. "How's your forehead?"

Boone lifted a hand and touched the spot above his eye. Nixie admired the way his simple motion caused the muscles to bunch in his upper arm. "Back to normal."

Slipping back into the role she'd played so many years ago, she shot back, "I knew that hard head of yours would come in handy some day."

Boone was just as quick with his response. "It's even harder now. I don't take no for an answer." He leaned forward, bracing his elbows on his knees. "I still feel bad about shrinking your dress. Let me take you to dinner Friday night.''

"That's not necessary. Besides, you've more than made up for it by buying Chad's uniform.''

"I would have done that anyway." He leaned back again and pushed back the shaggy blond hair that had fallen over his eyebrow. When Nixie started to make excuses, he repeated, ''I don't take no for an answer.''

Nixie studied the man who had once been her chief tormentor. Why was he being so nice now? This side of Boone Shelton unsettled her. She was used to dealing with his orneriness and teasing, aggravating as it was. But when he was being nice, like this, she couldn't help suspecting he was up to something.

She shook off the feeling of unease. Maybe he was truly repentant for what he'd done to her dress and was honestly trying to make it up to her. If that was the case, maybe she should let him assuage his guilt and be done with it.

"What if we just say it's for old times' sake?" he prompted.

Maybe if she said yes, he'd satisfy his guilt, she'd satisfy her belief that they could never get along, and then they'd both go their own separate ways. "I get off at five," she said, "unless I happen to be tending a hit-and-run victim.''

"That should be no problem since one of the Cub Scouts wrote down the license number of the car that hit me. The driver is to appear in court next month." He laughed. "Funny thing is, we had just talked at the meeting before that about what to do if you witness a crime. Those kids remember more than you'd think.''

There was no mistaking the pride in his voice when he talked about the young Scouts. A chill came over her as she realized that was the same tone Paul had used when bragging about Stephanie and Chad. At times such as this, Boone Shelton actually seemed tender and sensitive, an image that did not go with his boisterous, rough nature.

Dinner Friday night was another occasion in which Nixie was forced to look at her childhood nemesis in a different light.

She'd been expecting him to take her to the Rib Rack, a popular local restaurant that featured lots of beef and a casual—even rowdy—atmosphere. Instead he'd surprised her by making reservations at Jean Jacques. He'd surprised her further by recommending an excellent chicken dish to Nixie and ordering their meals in fluent French. This was certainly not the monosyllabic boy she remembered from high school.

As they waited for their dinner, Boone asked her a few questions and soon she was telling him all about Paul. Not just the good things that people tend to remember after a loved one is gone, but she even told him that her husband had been a workaholic, something she'd never shared with anyone else. When she described how they'd been on their way to a weekend getaway at a mountain cabin to escape the stress of his job and of tending to the two babies, she appreciated Boone's quiet understanding. And when she described how she had tried helplessly to free her unconscious husband from the flaming car after he'd fallen asleep at the wheel and crashed into a tree, she was thankful for Boone's nonpitying empathy.

It wasn't until their desserts arrived that she realized she had monopolized the entire conversation. "I'm sorry," she said. "I didn't mean to bore you."

Boone looked across the table at the exciting woman sitting opposite him. "You don't bore me." He wanted to add, "You fascinate me," but thought better of it. With his record of teasing, he knew she wouldn't take him seriously.

"Well, enough about me," she said, plunging her spoon into the strawberry parfait. "Tell me about your newspaper. You seem to be making quite a few improvements."

"There's not much to tell," he admitted. "I saw my hometown newspaper on the brink of going under, so I bought it and am trying to turn it around."

"I've been enjoying the new advice column, 'Ask Aunt Alice.' Is she a local person?"

Boone tensed. He bought a few seconds by mashing the remaining crumbs of his seven-layer cake onto his fork. "Alice is a very private person," he said at last. "She feels more comfortable staying in the background."

Nixie nodded her agreement. "I suppose it would get tiresome to have people telling her their problems every time she goes to the store or to get her hair done."

He smiled. "Yes, I suppose it's something like that."

Nixie dabbed the napkin to her mouth and flashed him a decidedly sneaky smile. "Do you always reserve the front page for catastrophic, earth-shaking news?"

Boone paused a moment before answering. From that smug smile to her intense interest in his plans for the newspaper, it was clear she was baiting him. Always open for a little sport, he bit. "Only the most incredible news goes on page one."

"Like the opossum that gave birth in Mrs. Masten's garbage can?"

"It's not every day a person finds baby wildlife in her garbage can."

"If the rescue squad were to sponsor a fund-raiser, would you put that on page one?"

Boone smiled his amusement. The woman was definitely persistent. "It depends on whether the photo opportunity rates right up there with Mrs. Masten's opossums."

"Just what I wanted to hear. I'm sure you'll want to assign a reporter to cover our project, as soon as I figure out what it's going to be. I'll let you know the date as soon as the committee decides."

"Tell me, why is it so important for the rescue squad to receive news coverage in the *Gazette?*"

"It's the fire department, too, actually. We're having membership drives, and public awareness makes people more willing to donate money to buy more modern equipment and convert to the Enhanced 911 system."

"What's wrong with the current system?"

"The emergency number is a local telephone number, which people frequently forget in a crisis. The enhanced 911 system is computerized and allows the dispatcher to see on a computer the address and telephone number of the citizen as soon as the call is made."

It seemed fairly obvious, but as a journalist he had to ask, "Why can't the caller give the address?"

A shadow fell over Nixie's delicate features. He knew from experience that she wasn't as delicate as she looked, but right now she seemed almost . . . fragile.

"A passerby called for help from a nearby pay phone after our car crashed. The directions he gave were unclear." Nixie grew silent for a moment before continuing. "Paul might have been saved if the fire department had arrived two or three minutes sooner."

Boone frowned and idly rubbed where the hair tickled the nape of his neck. She was blaming herself for her husband's death. No wonder she was so insistent in her efforts to publicize the rescue squad's activities.

He reached into his pocket and pulled out a pair of wire-rimmed glasses, then withdrew his ever-present pad and pen from his coat pocket. "This sounds like a story." Jotting down the essentials, he said, "I'll have the feature writer contact you next week."

Nixie was shaking her head. "I don't want a story about me. I'd be happier if you'd send your reporter to cover the squad's publicity project...when we pick a date for it, that is."

He figured now would be the time to tell her about the Cub Scout camp-out next month. "All right," he said, tucking the pad and pen back in his coat pocket, "but I'd suggest you make it any day but the twenty-fifth. That's the weekend of the family camporee."

Nixie looked at him blankly. It didn't sound like something that should concern her.

"The Cub Scout camp-out," Boone added. "Chad is expected to come. And you and Stephanie should be there that morning and afternoon for Family Day."

Nixie didn't like the idea of this. What had started as a few den meetings where her son would memorize pledges and make crafts had now ballooned into the kind of activity she feared for him to be involved in. Why, he could become lost in the woods, get bitten by a snake, or any number of other things she'd rather not think about.

Boone must have misread her concern for reluctance to participate. "You won't have to stay for the whole thing," he assured. "That night is for Scouts and fathers only."

Nixie didn't have time to respond before he caught his error and suggested, "Perhaps Mr. Cordaire would like to fill in this time."

The panic she'd felt a moment ago was now replaced by amusement at his suggestion. "Uncle Jim sleeping in a tent? He might go for it if you could promise him a portable TV that would pick up HBO." She shook her head. "Besides, his snoring would keep everyone else awake."

His elbows resting on the table and his fingers steepled, Boone was quiet for a moment. In that suit and those glasses, he looked almost...studious. Quite a different picture from the time he'd appeared at her door in shredded jeans and a shirt with the sleeves hacked off.

"Then, unless you or Chad object, I'd like for him to be with me that night."

On the surface, it sounded like a sweet offer, but Nixie couldn't allow it if he was doing it out of pity. And worse, what if Chad mistakenly read something into the situation? She couldn't allow her son to be hurt. In the short time he'd known Boone, he already seemed to idolize him.

"I don't think that's a good idea."

From the way he clenched his jaw and narrowed his eyes, Nixie knew her comment had been carelessly blunt. She hadn't meant to hurt him, but she couldn't allow her child to be hurt, either.

"Fine, but if you can't find someone else, my offer still stands. Chad's a Cub Scout now, Nixie, and I expect him to be there and participate fully, come hell or high water...or rescue squad publicity event."

His meaning was clear. He was warning her not to plan her media event for that day and use it as an excuse not to attend the camporee. But he should know by now that

he could no longer tease, cajole, or even threaten her into
bending to his will. Boone Shelton had always managed
to pop into her life at the most inconvenient times—such
as the time he ruined her date with Craig Curtis, the high
school hunk—and he never failed to create turmoil with
her well-laid plans.

Well, this time he wouldn't do it. She wouldn't let him.
Although Nixie was happy that Chad had found a friend
in Boone and that the Scout leader encouraged him to act
more responsibly, she was leery of Boone's intrusion into
their lives. After all, he was encouraging her son to participate in new and risky activities. Her worst fear was
that something terrible might happen to one of her children.

Tonight was Friday, and Boone wasn't expected to
come to the house until next Wednesday, when he picked
up Chad for the weekly den meeting. Maybe by then
she'd come up with a way to discourage her son—her
baby—from going on the camporee. He was so small and
vulnerable, and he needed to be protected from Boone's
good intentions.

Boone stood and walked around to her chair. As he
offered her a hand up to escort her from the restaurant,
he flashed her a warm smile that threatened to melt her
resolve.

A frightening thought flitted through her mind. Who
would protect *her* from Boone and his good intentions?

Chapter Four

The next morning Nixie was still wondering at her re-action to Boone when he'd stood on her front porch and said good-night. For what must have been one of the most insane moments of her life, she'd found herself wishing he would kiss her.

Instead, Uncle Jim had switched on the porch light and peeked out through one of the three small windowpanes in the door. Even if Boone had been inclined to kiss her, Nixie was certain that the sight of her grinning uncle would have been enough to squelch the notion.

She hadn't slept well and chose to blame her restlessness on the rich food she'd eaten at dinner. When she awoke early to the sound of water gurgling down the rainspout and thunder clapping in the distance, she got up and pitched her fitful energy into Saturday morning chores.

Chad dragged a broom from the utility room and started pushing it ineffectually around the dining room.

As Stephanie passed him with a dust rag in her hand, Nixie heard her grumble, "Do you think Mom was a drill sergeant in a former life?"

Chad nodded his agreement.

She had been working them hard this morning. But, as her parents had taught her and her brother, a little hard work never hurt anyone. Besides, once they were finished, they'd have the rest of the day to play. Nixie opened the dishwasher and started putting the clean dishes away. With a little smile, she ordered, "No talking in the ranks."

They obediently went about their work. A few minutes later, Stephanie came rushing into the kitchen. "Mom, there's a man in the bushes out front!"

Nixie put the last cup in the cabinet. "Honey, it's pouring outside. I don't think—" One look at her daughter's panicked face assured her that Stephanie had seen *something*. "It's probably just a neighbor's dog," she said. "Come show me where you saw it."

"See," Stephanie said as they pulled back the curtain, "he's down on all fours, and his shoes are sticking out from under the bush."

"Want me to get the gun?" Chad shouted.

"We don't have a gun. Go get your baseball bat."

The figure slowly backed out from under the bush. When he rose, Nixie could see that he was tall, even though he stood hunched against the rain. Through the downpour, it looked as though he were hiding something under his jacket. He turned and started toward the house.

By now Stephanie was in a panic. "I'm going to call Uncle Jim. He'll know what to do."

Chad returned with the baseball bat. "I'm going to go out the back door, sneak up on him, and bash him over the head!'' He swung the bat for emphasis and almost knocked over a lamp.

"No!" Nixie took the bat from her son. "Go make sure the door is locked. Stephanie, get off the phone in case we need to call the police."

"Uncle Jim's not home! What if that man tries to kill us?"

"Stephanie, get a grip," Nixie snapped. "Try to set a good example for Chad."

Chad, by now, was *un*locking the front door. He pulled it open and rushed out into the rain toward the stranger.

"Chad!" Nixie raced after him, the bat clutched tightly in her hand.

Just as her son reached him, the man looked up, his blue eyes smiling at Nixie.

"Kind of wet for a ball game, don't you think?"

Nixie's emotions warred between relief and indignation. "Boone, you almost scared the life out of us! What are you doing skulking around in my yard?"

"Getting wet." He opened one side of his jacket and enveloped Chad in it the way a hen would protect a chick with her wing. "Why don't we talk inside where it's more comfortable?"

Once inside, there was no opportunity for her to lay into him as she'd intended. There were towels to fetch and muddy shoes to contend with. And just when she was about to give Boone a piece of her mind, he removed a soggy bundle of brown fluff from inside his jacket and placed it on the floor.

The animal was so soiled and matted she could hardly tell what it was until it meowed. "Oh, my," said Nixie. "It's that stray cat that's been hanging around here for the past week."

Boone took a dry towel and wrapped it around the squirming kitten. "I saw it limping toward the bush when I drove up."

"Mom, its leg is hurt," said Stephanie. "Look, it's bleeding."

Nixie sighed and got up to retrieve the first-aid kit. "Don't get too attached to it," she told the kids. "We don't have room for another animal."

At their groans, Nixie realized the kitten would be easier to remove from their lives than the two-legged animal that had brought it in.

A short while later, its brown fur dried and the minor wound on its leg tended, the kitten slept in a cardboard box lined with an old blanket.

Nixie looked over at the big man who dominated her couch. Though he was older and small lines marked the corners of his eyes, he was still protecting those smaller than himself.

Boone watched with interest as she repacked the antibiotic cream in the carrying case and snapped the lid shut. "Why do you keep clean underwear in your first-aid kit?"

Nixie smiled as she thought of her son's goofy sense of humor. "Chad put them there in case he gets hurt and has to go to the hospital."

Boone turned to Chad and nudged the boy with his elbow. "Did you get tired of your mom's lectures?"

Chad gave his new pal a beleaguered look that said more clearly than words, "Women!"

Although she was the subject of their shared joke, Nixie was glad to see that her mischievous son admired such a solid, stable role model as Boone. Even though Boone was somewhat pushy about urging her to let Chad become more involved in Scouting, it was clear that his intentions were good and that he could be a good influence on a boy.

Remembering their conversation of last night, she wondered if he had come to pressure her into letting Chad go on the camporee. Due to her lack of sleep last night, she doubted her sluggish mind could quickly come up with a reasonable excuse to keep the boy home, where he'd be safe.

"Your ears must be bionic if you heard that cat's distress call all the way from your apartment," Nixie told him.

"Actually," he said, brandishing two envelopes, "I came to deliver these. Forgot to give them to Stephanie and Chad yesterday," he added.

"Letters?" Stephanie stopped rubbing the kitten and stepped closer to Boone.

"Somebody answered our ad!" Chad crowed.

Nixie shot Boone a look that should have withered his socks, but he just grinned back at her.

She had to give him credit, though. Before he let them open the envelopes, he talked about how they shouldn't get their hopes up if someone sounded good in a letter, and they shouldn't be discouraged if the respondents weren't suitable. "There are all kinds of people out there," he told them, "and you take a risk when you ask them to correspond with you."

"I'm going in the other room," Nixie announced. "I want nothing to do with this." Nevertheless, she found herself loitering near the archway leading into the living room, where she could hear all that was said.

"She'll come around," Chad said. "All we gotta do is find her a good one."

Boone moved over so there was room for a child to sit on either side of him. Out of the corner of his eye, he could see Nixie making a pretense of wiping fingerprints off the wall.

"Okay," he told the kids, "let's see what this one says." He unfolded the letter, and they read it together.

I don't write good but if you wud call me I wil tell you all abot myself.

A phone number was included under the sloppily scrawled signature.

"What do you think?" he asked them.

Stephanie was quick to offer her opinion. "Not!"

Chad shrugged. "He can't spell, but maybe he's a nice person."

"He's not the one for us." Stephanie was insistent. "How could he help us with our homework? And I don't think Mom would go for him because she'd want someone who reads a lot. People who read usually spell better than people who don't read."

"Good point," said Boone. He balled up the letter.

"What about the other one?" Chad asked.

"This one sounds better," Boone told them. He read it aloud so Nixie could hear.

I was interested in your advertisement because I'm very lonely and want to share in the love of a close family relationship. Realizing that no one is perfect, I would accept you just as you are. I ask only that you afford me the same courtesy. I believe family members should talk to each other every day, and I look forward to planning some wonderful family activities with you. Please write soon. If you don't, I'll be patient. I have plenty of time.

Chad grabbed the letter. "Hey, he sounds pretty good."

Boone noticed that Nixie had stopped what she was doing to listen.

Stephanie was looking at the return address on the envelope. "What does 1988476 mean?"

Boone studied the envelope a moment. "That's his prison number."

"Boone, may I speak with you in here?" Nixie thrummed her fingers on the wall she'd just wiped down.

When he came into the dining room, Nixie had to tilt her head back to look up at him. That didn't keep her from shaking a finger at him as if he were one of her own children. "That's exactly why I didn't want them to go through with this foolishness!"

"Don't worry, Nix." Boone grabbed her hand and curled her index finger down with the rest. "Those kids are smart enough not to get you hooked up with a felon."

"How do you know he's a felon?"

"Return address," he replied. "He's in the maximum security unit."

"Oh, good grief!"

Quietly, so that only she could hear, he leaned closer and murmured in her ear, "Wouldn't it be simpler to forget about finding a stranger to fill the position and start looking at candidates you know?"

Nixie almost stopped breathing. Was he recommending himself? Or was it just wishful thinking on her part? She had to get a grip on herself. Maybe Aunt Laura was right . . . maybe she'd been too long without a man in her life. Maybe, too, she was subconsciously trying to fill that void with someone safe and familiar.

He was certainly familiar, but Nixie doubted she was safe around him. For all she knew, his comment could have been another teasing joke. Well, she'd play along.

"Yes, you're probably right," she admitted. "Let's see, there's old Mr. Finch who cleans our offices every week. Why, did you know he's expecting his fourteenth grandchild next month? Such a dear man. And so lonely since his Clara passed away."

She casually rubbed another fingerprint from the wall. He was playing hardball, refusing to grant her even a glimmer of a smile as he pretended to believe her.

"Then there's always Markey Evans down the block," she continued. "He's only sixteen, but I hear he has incredible buns."

"Mom!" cried Stephanie. "You don't have to go and tell everyone what I said."

Precious, who had earlier run terrorized from the room when Chad had pretended to "sweep" her with the broom, now returned and noticed the little brown furball trying to climb out of its box. Though normally timid, the older cat crept closer to the box, hissed loudly, and took a swat at the tiny intruder.

All four humans leapt to the kitten's defense, and Precious was quickly banished to the utility room. Stephanie was visibly shaken by her pet's uncharacteristic display of hostility. "Precious is usually so sweet. Why would she try to hurt that innocent little kitten?"

Nixie put an arm around her daughter. "I'm sure she wasn't trying to hurt the kitten. She was just trying to protect her domain."

"Her domain?"

"Yes. Her turf. Precious considers this house her own. And when a new animal comes in, it feels like that animal is invading her territory."

"It's my fault," said Boone. "I shouldn't have brought it in here. I'll take it to the pound when I leave. Since it's so young, maybe someone will adopt it."

"And maybe they won't," Stephanie declared.

Chad grabbed Boone's arm. "Why don't you take it home with you?"

Nixie tried to imagine the kitten living in that stark, bachelor apartment. It would be alone all day while Boone worked. And Boone probably worked overtime occasionally, not to mention the time that he spent with the Scouts.

Boone slowly shook his head. "Sorry, pal. It just wouldn't work out."

Pushing aside her earlier comment about not having enough room for another animal, Nixie impulsively blurted out, "It's going to need medical attention until that leg heals. We may as well let it stay here so I can keep an eye on it."

The kids exploded with cheers, and Boone shot her his familiar teasing grin. "You always were a soft touch," he said.

He was grinning, but the way he said it made her think about soft touches...*his* soft touches on her heated body. If she weren't careful, he'd have her blushing like the shy teenager she used to be.

"I guess I'll let y'all get back to your housework," he said, heading for the door. His hand on the knob, he stopped and turned to Chad. "I expect to see you at the family camporee next weekend."

For the next week, Chad could talk of nothing else. Nixie had reluctantly agreed to let him go, but she frequently quizzed him with what-if scenarios to prepare him for an emergency. By the end of the week, she'd taught him what to do in case he got bitten by a snake, lost in the woods, cut or otherwise injured. Still not satisfied, she came up with several uncommon scenarios so he'd be prepared for those, too.

At Nixie's urging, Chad asked Jim to accompany him on the camp-out, but the older man declined, saying his bad back needed the comfort of his bed at home.

She thought of asking her younger brother to spend the weekend with Chad, but Ryan's wife was due to deliver their first child at any time.

Chad settled the issue after returning home from his weekly den meeting. Nixie smiled at her son in his navy blue uniform. He was so proud of being a Scout, he'd started wearing it to school on the day of the meeting, claiming he didn't have enough time to change after school. He wouldn't even hold Tarzan on meeting days for fear the bird might soil the shirt.

"Mom, guess what?" he said, slamming his Scout manual down on the kitchen table and raiding the cookie jar. "I asked Boone to be my dad for the weekend when we go camping."

Nixie stiffened. This was just what she had feared would happen. Chad had often said he wished he had a father like other kids did. He'd even pretended sometimes that Jim was his father.

What if her son transferred his need for a strong male figure to Boone? Boone had moved away from Lakewood once. He could do it again. "What did Boone say?" Nixie prompted, praying he'd had the foresight not to build up the boy's hopes.

Chad shrugged and munched his cookie. "He said no one could take the place of my real dad, but that he would be my mentor—whatever that is."

Nixie's heart seemed to lodge in her throat. Boone hadn't changed a bit. After he'd antagonized her until she thought she couldn't stand it any more, he would do something endearing like this. She supposed that was the only reason they'd managed to maintain a semblance of friendship during their school years.

"Can I take Tarzan with me on the camping trip?"

"Absolutely not."

By the time Saturday came, Stephanie was dead set against going. "I don't see why I have to go to Chad's dumb Scout camp."

Nixie gave her daughter a look that warned her not to start an argument in front of company.

Boone picked up Chad's sleeping bag to take it to his car. "Look on the bright side," he told her. "You might meet some cute older Scouts." He tugged her ponytail and went out the door, Chad close on his heels.

Nixie reached into the refrigerator for the last juice box that had been pushed to the back, then dumped ice into the cooler. "We're just going to be there for the day. It's a family thing."

"Well, I don't see why we couldn't ask Uncle Jim and Aunt Laura to come," she retorted. "Boone's not family."

"Uncle Jim and Aunt Laura are in town shopping for a new living room set. Now, stop arguing and be a good sport."

As Nixie and Stephanie carried the cooler to the front door, Nixie noticed Boone and Chad had returned and were standing in front of the bird cage.

"Nice bird," Boone said as Nixie approached. He turned to the green and red feathered chatterbox and said, "I've heard your Tarzan yodel and your giggle. Can you talk?"

The children looked at each other. Nixie could tell they were thrilled Boone had set himself up for the smart-alecky reply that was sure to come. Chad had taught it to the bird for just such an occasion. She smiled as she anticipated Boone's surprise.

Tarzan cocked his head and peered up at Boone. "I can talk," the bird quipped in its croaky voice. "Can you fly?"

The children burst into hysterical laughter. Boone stepped back from the cage and stared open-mouthed at the green joker. The wing flapping and the long-winded laugh that Tarzan graced him with made it seem as if he, too, were amused.

"What's the matter?" Nixie goaded. "Haven't you ever had a conversation with a bird before?" She loved dishing out the teasing for a change.

Boone caught her eye, and it was clear he planned to get even. No matter. The shocked expression on his face was worth whatever mischievous deed he had planned for her.

His face a mask of pure innocence, Boone turned to Chad and asked, "How long does it take him to learn something new?"

"About a week or two," Chad said proudly. "Sometimes quicker if he thinks what you're teaching him sounds interesting."

Nixie reminded them of the time, and each picked up something to carry to the car. All but Boone. He was still standing in front of the cage, muttering something to the bird. When he caught Nixie watching him, he joined the rest of them in the foyer and picked up the cooler. "I was just telling him goodbye."

"Have a birdiful day!" Tarzan sang out.

Boone gave her a puzzled glance. "How does he do that?"

"Do what?"

"Know when to say things."

Pleased to have witnessed his being caught off guard for the second time that morning, Nixie just smiled and said, "Sometimes I think he's the smartest one in the family."

The camporee was being held at a nearby state park. Nixie and Stephanie set up the picnic while Boone and the other Scout leaders taught the young charges how to erect their tents. As they waited for the boys to finish, she and Stephanie explored the area.

Nixie was glad to see the park wasn't as "uncivilized" as she'd anticipated. The picnic tables where they would have lunch were protected by a shelter, and although it was too cool for swimming, the small man-made lake would provide good fishing for the boys. A nearby bath house offered running water. A clearing in the woods sported rough, split-log benches placed in a semicircle around a large backdrop of plyboard painted white. Here the boys could gather for movies tonight and for church in the morning. Nixie was also pleased to note that the ranger's shack was less than a mile away. She'd have to remember to tell Chad that in case of an emergency, he could call her from there.

After the Scouts came back from setting up their tents and ate lunch, there wasn't time for anyone to get bored. Boone's den and interested family members went horseback riding while others separated to go fishing or hiking. An avid horse lover, Stephanie ceased griping for the duration of the trail ride.

On their return to the barn, one of Nixie's fears came true. Roger, a boy whose father had not been able to attend and who would also be sharing a tent with Boone, got stung by a bee. While Nixie examined the red, swollen area on the boy's wrist, Chad ran to get his knapsack.

"I'll take care of it," Chad announced. He seemed eager to prove that he was able to handle this minor crisis, just as he and Nixie had rehearsed at home.

Nixie stepped back and watched as her son retrieved a small tube containing a greenish solution and dabbed the sponge tip to Roger's skin.

Boone sidled up to her. "You should be proud of Chad. He's good Scout material." He absentmindedly rubbed his arm, and Nixie noted the strength in it. "He's a mechanical whiz, too. Put that tent up before I finished explaining how to do it."

His compliment warmed her, probably more than if it had come from someone else. She was, indeed, proud of her son . . . and he didn't have to erect a pup tent or tend a bee sting to inspire that feeling. He was a great kid purely on his own merits. She still didn't feel comfortable leaving him this weekend, and Roger's run-in with the horsefly made her even more nervous.

"Looks like Roger was bee bait," she said a bit more harshly than she intended. "I just hope Chad won't be bear bait."

Boone put an arm around her shoulder. It was a brotherly gesture, but it created sensations deep inside her. It made her feel safe and secure, as if his strong arms could protect her from any danger. "Chad's a smart kid who can watch out for himself," he said. "And even if he doesn't, I will."

His assurance helped some, but not enough.

"I forgot to tell him what to do if he comes across a rabid raccoon."

Boone squeezed her shoulder. *"Don't worry."*

"That's easy for you to say," she muttered.

"Tell you what," he said. "How do you feel about giving a short first-aid lesson to the boys? You could help some of them earn a badge," he urged.

Nixie knew he was trying to divert her attention away from the potential dangers that existed for her son. She let him. It was too frustrating to keep imagining the worst.

Boone threw his head back and laughed out loud. Nixie Thomas's kid was a hoot.

As they had settled down around the campfire to toast their marshmallows, one of the boys started the age-old tradition of telling scary stories. It wasn't long before little Roger was frightened out of his wits. That was when Chad started telling funny anecdotes about his Uncle Jim's pranks. Jim's antics were funny, but the kid's storytelling ability was even funnier.

Before long, Roger's fears were quieted and he was trying to top the others with his own wacky tales.

Boone's eyes were drawn back to Chad. In the flickering firelight, the boy's small features and infectious smile reminded him of Nixie. Unlike his mother, however, Chad had a dimple in his right cheek and wispy blond hair. A small, vertical scar from an earlier mishap was evident on the left side of his chin. The boy was sure to be a ladykiller. Boone only hoped Chad wouldn't be as shy and awkward around girls as Boone had been around Nixie.

Boone hadn't had the benefit of his father's experience and advice because his parents had divorced shortly before his mother brought them to Lakewood to live. His father hadn't visited or even kept up support payments. Boone had to hand it to his mother for never once calling the guy a bum. Which he was.

And now Chad didn't have benefit of a father's advice. Boone chuckled as he recalled the day the two youngsters had come into his office and informed him they wanted to place an ad for a daddy.

If it had been his choice, he would have been their daddy from the start. He'd planned to graduate from college, get his career established, and go back to Lakewood to pursue Nixie in earnest. But, as he'd prepared to enter his third year of college, his sister had written in one of her regular letters that the girl who'd stolen his heart had already married someone else.

He couldn't blame Nixie. He'd teased her so ruthlessly she'd probably been glad to see him go.

He'd been so distraught, he went to a college hangout, met Cheryl, and proposed within six months. The marriage had lasted less than two years.

Maybe, if he didn't screw things up this time, he could have another chance with Nixie. He smiled. Maybe, someday, he'd offer fatherly advice to the kid at his elbow and spare him the same grief he'd known.

He playfully grabbed Chad by the back of the neck, gave a light squeeze, and whispered in his ear, "Better get in the tent before the vampire bats come out."

Later, after they'd settled into their sleeping bags, Chad and Roger started telling him about school, their pets and the latest stock-car race Chad had watched on television. Boone made a mental note to take the boys to the races on one of their future outings.

"What was that noise?" Roger whispered.

Boone listened. At first, all he could hear was crickets chirping and the murmuring from fathers and sons in nearby tents. Then he heard the distinctive sound of dried leaves and twigs crackling.

"Maybe it's a raccoon," Chad suggested.

It was bigger than a raccoon, Boone was certain, but he didn't want to scare the boys. "Maybe." He got up and opened the tent flap. "I'm going to take a look."

He'd forgotten the flashlight, but the moon was full so he could make out the dim shadows of rounded pup tents and nearby trees.

Leaves rustled again, and he turned to the source of the noise. The shape lurking behind a tree was definitely not animal. Boone's first thought was that one of the campers had answered nature's call, but the figure seemed too small for a father and too large for a Scout.

He moved closer, wishing he'd thought to bring his knife. For all he knew, it could be someone trying to harm the unwary campers. When he realized he couldn't get any closer without the intruder hearing or spotting him, he made a tackle that would have been the envy of any semi-pro football player.

The high-pitched scream that followed nearly deafened him.

Chapter Five

"Boone, what is it?" Chad called out. "Are you all right?"

At first Boone thought he imagined the soft curves beneath him, but when he caught scent of the floral perfume that was her trademark, Boone knew it could be no one other than Nixie.

Flashlight beams danced around them as a couple of fathers came to see what all the commotion was about.

"It's okay," Boone told them. "It's just a hiker who got lost. Everything's under control."

He only wished everything *was* under control. His body was betraying him badly, and Nixie's squirming was making it worse.

Thankfully, the men went back to their respective tents and Chad had apparently accepted his explanation of what was happening. Boone turned his attention back to Nixie. He didn't move off her but just raised up on his hands and hovered over her.

"Don't you think it's late for a hike?"

The sound that came out of her was close to a growl. Boone couldn't help thinking he'd like to try to elicit a moan. But Nixie quickly let him know he could forget that notion.

"Are you going to get off me, or do I have to use what I learned in self-defense class?"

Boone laughed. From her position, she could do little more than wiggle and squirm, and those were *not* good self-defense measures. He got up and helped her to her feet. He let his hand linger at her waist and was pleased when she didn't step away.

"Let me guess," he persisted. "You were thinking about the daddy candidates and decided to come ask me to apply for the position."

She lowered her head. "Boone, quit teasing. I already feel silly enough as it is."

With the back of his knuckle, he gently stroked her chin until she looked up at him. "What makes you think I'm teasing?"

She grew silent for a long moment, long enough for Boone to think she might take him up on his offer to apply for the job of daddy to her children. For a brief instant, he dared to hope.

"I—I was worried about Chad," she said softly. "I wanted to make sure he's all right."

His hopes dashed, Boone let out his breath in a puff of disappointment.

Apparently reading the sound as a snort of disgust, Nixie stepped out of his grasp and turned away from him. "I figured you wouldn't understand. But that's okay. I'm used to your kind of attitude." She stepped past him and moved toward the tent. "I'll just take a peek at Chad, tell him good night, and leave."

Boone reached out for her, his fingers closing around her tiny wrist. "No."

Nixie hesitated, then tried to pull her arm away from him. When he didn't relax his grip, she must have realized the futility of struggling with him and stood still. Even in the darkness, Boone could see her straighten her shoulders the way she used to do whenever she was on the losing end of an argument. "No?"

He lowered his voice. "You show your face in that camp tonight, and your son won't be able to show his face in school next week." Still gripping her wrist, he pulled her to him and gently patted her arm. "I know you don't want to make him the laughingstock of all his friends, but that's exactly what would happen if anyone finds out you were here tonight."

She turned and looked toward the camp, needing to be assured that her little boy was safe and happy.

"Come on," he said. "I'll walk you to your car."

Someone unzipped the tent flap and stepped outside. "Whatcha doing, Boone?"

Nixie instinctively made a step toward her son, then stopped.

Boone motioned for Nixie to stay where she was while he went to the tent to retrieve his forgotten flashlight. "Go back inside and stay there," he told Chad. "I'm going to take the hiker back to the parking area."

The boy went back into the tent as directed and let out a big laugh. "Hey, Roger, can you believe some dork is out hiking at this time of night!"

Boone smiled as he rezipped the tent flap. With the flashlight beam to light their path, he started walking with Nixie at his side. After that comment, he doubted Nixie would ever let on that she'd been here tonight. "He's going to be all right, you know."

She walked beside him in silence.

"Where's Stephanie?" he asked.

Nixie took his hand as they stepped over a root. "She's spending the night at my aunt and uncle's." They walked a little farther before they reached the asphalt. "My car is parked over there, near yours."

He held his hand out for her keys and unlocked the vehicle for her. It was small, like its owner, the lines sleek and slightly rounded. He wondered if she'd chosen the rich, cream color because it complemented the hint of flame in her brown hair.

He shone the flashlight's beam over the back seat and floorboards, then started to move aside for her to get in. At the last moment, he impulsively blocked her path.

"Chad's having a good time. Don't worry about him."

She let out a small breath that sounded like an attempt at a laugh. "That's easier said than done."

Boone reached up and touched the dark strand of hair that caressed her cheek. He pushed the hair back and took the honor himself, trailing his fingers over the soft, fair skin. "What can I do to reassure you?"

It was hard to tell what happened next. Did he pull her to him, or did she move toward him first and lay her head on his chest? It didn't matter. What mattered was that she was finally where she belonged . . . in his arms.

He held her, but not so tight she'd pull away. His touch was gentle, even lighter than he'd used when rescuing the kitten. He didn't want to scare her away, not when she'd finally allowed him to be strong for her.

Years ago, he'd wanted to be her protector. He'd wanted to take care of her the way she tried to take care of others. Nixie had so much love to give, and he wanted her to share it with him. But she'd been so busy trying to be the strong one—the one who visited the elderly at the retirement home, who tutored the slow learners, and who organized fund-raisers for the less fortunate.

Now, fifteen years later, she was still trying to be the strong one—for her children, in her business, and for her rescue victims. He wanted to show her she didn't have to be strong all the time. She could be vulnerable . . . and soft . . . and feminine . . . Boone's hands moved over the baggy windbreaker that covered her slight frame.

She lifted her face to look at him.

In the warm glow that shone from the car's interior light, he saw the fear in her eyes. He suspected the fear came not so much from concern over her son's well-being, but from the knowledge that she could not protect those she loved from the dangers of everyday life. She was afraid of not being in control.

He lowered his head and touched his mouth to the sweet lips that had taunted him since his youth. The lips that had grown fuller, redder, and more inviting with time. His hand coursed down to the small of her waist and pulled her closer to him, as if that small action could somehow bring him the satisfaction he needed.

Nixie pressed closer, her small breasts pushing against his torso in welcome invitation. His body responded to the invitation and sought to fill the physical and emotional void in this woman who had haunted his soul since before he was old enough to give girls a second look.

They shifted, and she was against the car, moving her backside slowly up and down along the metal. Boone's knee came up between her thighs, and he explored the sweetness of her mouth with his tongue. The gesture didn't still her movements, but seemed to encourage them.

It was as if they couldn't get close enough to one another. But if they got any closer, there'd be no turning back. Boone raised his head and looked down at the woman who seemed to need him as much as he needed her.

Her eyes were heavy-lidded with desire, and her breath came in ragged pants, as did his own. Only a moment ago her hands had clutched his shoulders; now they relaxed and rested in a loop behind his neck.

"Wow," she said. "You sure do know how to reassure a person."

He laughed, tightened his arms around her until her feet no longer touched the ground, and turned them both around in a carefree spin. He planted a light kiss on her swollen lips. "If you don't go home now," he warned, "we're going to end up spending the whole night out here. And I don't think Chad or Roger would be happy about that."

Nixie moved to get in her car, then hesitated. "Boone?" she said.

He looked at her, knowing that if she didn't leave soon he'd be tempted to take her in the back seat. And he wanted their first time together to be more special than that. "Yes?"

"Thanks."

He grinned. "Anytime."

"For taking good care of Chad, I mean."

"Sure. That, too."

Nixie was going to wring his neck. Boone wouldn't blame her if she did. After all that talk about taking care of Chad, here he was bringing her son home in this condition.

Boone flipped down the visor to shade his eyes from the midafternoon sun. He glanced over at the boy riding shotgun in the seat beside him. Chad gave him a lop-sided grin and started giggling uncontrollably.

"Ish it kinda hot in here?" Chad slurred. He reached for the air-conditioning control and almost toppled over, but he was restrained by the seat belt across his chest.

"I'll get it." Boone cranked up the air conditioner and aimed a vent at Chad. It was bad enough the kid was going home this way. He didn't want him getting sick, too.

Boone scratched the stubble that had sprouted overnight on his chin.

How was he going to tell Nixie her son was drunk?

Minutes later, he was pulling up in Nixie's driveway. Boone wished he'd had a couple of hours to take Chad to his apartment and let him sleep it off before he came home. But Nixie was expecting them, and she'd worry if he wasn't home on time.

He killed the engine and walked around to open Chad's door. The boy was asleep, his cheek resting against the fabric seat belt.

"Come on, Sleeping Beauty," Boone told him. "It's time to own up to our misdeeds."

Chad roused, but only slightly, so Boone scooped him up and carried him toward the house. Just as he'd feared, Nixie saw her son and assumed the worst.

"What's the matter with him?" she demanded. "How did he get sick? Is it food poisoning, sun poisoning, what?"

"Let's get him inside. Then I'll explain everything."

Chad was soon settled on the couch. Boone, Nixie and Stephanie stood in a semicircle around him and watched as he tried to open his eyes and keep them open.

Boone turned to Stephanie. "Would you get your brother a bucket, honey? In case he...you know, barfs."

She glared at him, her expression almost as fearsome as her mother's. "Chad *never* gets sick," she declared, and huffed off to get the bucket.

Nixie knelt down and felt her son's forehead for fever. "What happened to Chad?" she demanded.

"Well, uh..." To stop himself from fidgeting, Boone shoved his hands in his pockets. There was no delicate way of putting it, so he may as well say it right out. "He sorta got a little bit looped."

Nixie stood up stiffly and turned to face Boone. He couldn't remember ever seeing her this angry. Her voice, when she finally responded, was soft, but far from gentle.

"My son is *drunk?*"

Chad stirred and said, "We played shug-lug."

Nixie turned to Boone. "Shug-lug?"

"He, uh, means chug-a-lug." He grinned as he remembered the silly game they had played before they left camp. "We had a little contest to see who would make the bottom of their juice box slurp first."

Stephanie came back into the room and placed the bucket on the floor near her brother.

"Where," said Nixie, "did Chad get alcohol?"

"Chad's drunk?" Stephanie turned and gave Boone another evil glare. "Mom," she said, "if he keeps on like this, he'll be in jail by the time he's ten."

Nixie pointed up the stairs. "Stephanie, go to your room."

The girl made a sullen exit. "Why don't you send Boone to his room?" she called down the stairs. "*He's* the one who got Chad drunk."

Boone cringed, but her reaction was understandable. He would have felt the same way if he'd been in Stephanie's shoes.

"Why don't we go in the kitchen and talk," he suggested, "while we make him a pot of coffee."

"No fair!" Stephanie called down the stairs. "I never get to drink coffee."

Nixie rolled her eyes and followed him into the kitchen. "What did he drink?"

Boone thought a moment. "Wine cooler, I suppose."

"You suppose? You don't know? Where did he get this wine cooler?"

He reached up and rubbed the spot in front of his ear. "From you."

Nixie almost dropped the coffeepot, and Boone leapt to catch it. She was handling this better than he'd expected. He put the glass pot under the drip mechanism. Walking over to the table, he pulled out a chair for her.

"Remember those juice boxes you sent?" At her affirmative nod, he continued. "One of them had apparently been in the refrigerator awhile and had fermented. After Chad started getting goofy, I checked the date on the box. It had expired a long time ago."

He watched the emotions that came and went on her face. She'd gone from anger to disbelief to something that looked like guilt.

"Oh, my gosh," she said, whacking her palm against her forehead. "That must have been the one that had been pushed to the back of the refrigerator. I thought the box seemed a little puffy, but I was in such a hurry I didn't look at it closely."

"Don't blame yourself." Boone reached across the table to cover her hand with his own. "I should have suspected something when Chad said his juice tasted 'tingly.'"

Nixie sighed heavily and buried her face in her hands. Boone wished there was something he could do or say to make the situation better.

Her shoulders were shaking now. Boone wanted to dry her tears and comfort her, but he didn't. Considering the mood she was in, he wouldn't be surprised if she used that self-defense move she'd threatened him with last night.

Then, to his surprise, he realized that her muffled sounds were laughter. Her shoulders shook harder, and she lifted her face until her eyes met his. She wiped a tear from the corner of her eye and giggled again.

"It's so ironic," she said. "I prepared him for snake-bites, broken bones, cuts, bee stings, getting lost, and everything else I could think of. Never once did it cross my mind to teach him how to identify alcoholic drinks or what to do in case he drank too much."

Boone got up, poured a cup of coffee, and handed it to Nixie. When she started to get up to take it to Chad, he stopped her. "No. It's for you. The best thing Chad can do right now is sleep. Here," he said, passing some sugar for her coffee, "you need it more than he does."

He poured himself a cup and joined her. "There's no way you can anticipate everything. All you can do is exactly what you've already done . . . prepare him the best way you know how, then pray he'll have the good sense to use what you've taught him so that he can take care of himself."

Nixie ran a finger around the rim of her cup. "It's so hard, wondering if the things I try to teach him actually sink in. He's so . . . giddy sometimes."

"You don't have anything to worry about," Boone assured her. "He wasn't giddy when he was treating Roger's bee sting, was he?" When she shook her head, he continued. "And he wasn't giddy this morning when he cooked his own eggs over the campfire."

She sat upright, and her spoon clattered on the table. "You let him near an open fire?"

"Yes, and his eggs looked so good I let him make some for me." He realized it was difficult for her to loosen the apron strings, but for Chad's sake she must. "He's going to grow up whether you like it or not. Wouldn't it be better to supervise him when he tries new things than to keep denying him and take a chance that he'll sneak behind your back to do it?"

She didn't respond, but Boone knew he'd given her something to think about.

"Why don't you go try to sober Chad up, and I'll dilute some coffee with milk and take it to Stephanie."

"I don't let the children drink coffee. Except when they're drunk," she amended. "The caffeine's bad for them."

Boone flashed her a winsome smile. "If I were you, I'd make an exception this time. Unless, of course, you want her thinking she has to get potted in order to sample it."

Upstairs, Stephanie didn't have much to say—just sat there on her bed, sipping coffee—so he chatted about a little of this, a little of that. She answered his questions with a nod or shake of the head. Anything else he asked was met with a sullen shrug. It was only when he mentioned the new kitten, Stormy, that she gave him more than a one-word response.

"Stormy is an intruder in Precious's domain," she said, quoting her mother. "He has to be kept in the utility room to keep from being attacked." She paused a moment, as if something had just occurred to her. "There are enough animals in this family for us to love. We didn't need any more."

Boone had a suspicion she wasn't talking just about the animals. "If you don't want Stormy, I can put an ad in my paper and try to find him a new home."

She looked up from her cup. "Mom said we should wait a while to see if Precious will learn to accept him. But I don't think she will," she added fatalistically. "Precious knows I love her, and she doesn't want to share me with anyone else."

Boone stood and patted the girl on the knee. "Give her some time. She'll come around."

As he left the room, he saw that she was shaking her head.

Downstairs, he found that Chad was up and around. The boy was standing by the bird cage, burping for all he was worth. The bird roamed free on top of the cage and seemed more than mildly interested in the strange noises coming from its owner. Nixie strode into the room with another cup of coffee and handed it to her son.

"If you're going to teach Tarzan to burp," she told the blond-haired rascal, "at least teach him to say 'excuse me' afterward."

Neither had seen Boone descend the steps. He stood at the bottom, leaning against the curved handrail, watching them . . . and enjoying what he saw. This family obviously loved each other, accepting the personality quirks of each without question. Boone liked that Nixie didn't try to shame her son into using better manners. She merely accepted that he was being playful, and she was willing to compromise.

That attitude was totally different from his ex-wife's. Cheryl had come into their marriage with expectations that opposed Boone's in almost every way. She hadn't wanted children, for instance. That was the big one.

The other things Boone probably could have lived with. Such as her compulsion about having a spotless house at all times. He'd never forget the time he tracked in mud after a touch football game with the neighborhood teens. Or the time he suggested they go canoeing. She'd just had her hair and nails done, she reminded him, and she had no desire to wallow in a dirty river with fish and bugs and snakes.

Even that he could have lived with. But they both knew their marriage was doomed the day he brought home half a dozen Scouts for their first weekly den meeting. He'd been so excited about starting a Scouting group where there had previously been none, and he was enthusiastic about making a positive impact on the young lives. When he explained to Cheryl how much Scouting had helped him grow emotionally and become more confident, he'd been sure she'd accept their presence for an hour and a half each week.

But she hadn't. While Boone was still glowing over the success of his first den meeting, Cheryl had insisted that he not bring "those disgusting little brats" back to their home.

And, now, here was Nixie, tolerating her son's disgusting noises with an amused smile. This was a close and loving family, and Boone wanted to be part of it.

After his conversation with Stephanie, though, he knew he'd have to tread softly.

He stepped into the living room. "Are you feeling better, Chad?"

"A little. Mom said the juice must not have been very potent if I bounced back this quick." He put emphasis on the word *potent,* as if he liked using what he considered an adult word.

"Glad to hear it," Boone said, smiling at Nixie. He was also glad to see that she smiled back at him. Maybe she wouldn't hold the incident against him after all.

"Hey, Mom," said Chad, "can I cook my breakfast tomorrow morning? Boone says I make some mean scrambled eggs."

She glanced again at Boone before answering. "We'll see," she said noncommittally.

"And Boone has this Scout pin that he's had since the olden days when he was a kid!"

"It's not exactly antique," Boone said with a grin, "but it is old. Here, you can wear it until I leave, if you want. Just don't lose it." He took it off and handed it to the boy, who turned the metal ornament over in his hands and admired the piece.

"I'm going to take Tarzan up to my room," he announced. "He likes to play with my toys." And then he was gone.

Nixie watched her son's departure. He took the steps a little more slowly than usual, but she was relieved to see that he hadn't been strongly affected by the fermented juice. She would have never forgiven herself if he'd had more than the mild reaction he'd suffered.

When she turned her attention back to her guest, she was unnerved to find him studying her. She wondered if he thought Chad was crude for burping at the bird. It must certainly reflect poorly on the way she was bringing up her son. And Boone certainly had opinions about other areas of the boy's upbringing.

"He's not usually that rude," she ventured. "I do teach the children good manners."

"It shows," he agreed. "They're good kids."

Nixie looked up at the handsome man who was now absentmindedly jiggling the bell hanging from Tarzan's cage. She wasn't surprised that her son was fond of him. She worried, though, that Chad might become too attached to him and get hurt. After all, there was no guarantee that he'd stay in Lakewood. Or even that he wouldn't meet someone nice, fall in love, get married, and have a family of his own.

For some inexplicable reason, that last thought made her uneasy. If he did get married and drop out of their lives, Chad wouldn't be the only one hurt.

Nixie was amazed at how quickly Boone had found a place in their family... and in their hearts. She had always been fond of him, even when he had tormented her with his endless teasing. And, though she tried to deny it, she'd missed him when he moved away from Lakewood after graduating from high school.

Maybe that was why she'd fallen so head-over-heels for Paul and married him shortly after they'd finished school. Her friends had told her Paul reminded them of Boone. She hadn't seen it, then; now she finally admitted that her husband's blond good looks and his gentle teasing were what had turned her head... the very qualities that had annoyed her in Boone.

To her, it had seemed as though Boone's looks were merely a tool for attracting girls, for he certainly must have had a black book chock-full of names. And although his teasing had been tiresome at the time, it had pleased her to be the focus of his attention.

To be truthful, Nixie liked having Boone back in her life. Although he still frustrated her with his joking and needling, Nixie found that she was becoming less resentful of his intrusion into the family's affairs and more eager to see him during his frequent visits.

Not that she was taking his overtures too seriously. She was well aware that even though he'd practically knocked her socks off last night, it had most likely been little more than a mild flirtation to him.

Even so, she couldn't keep from blurting out, "Stephanie's ballet recital is next Saturday. Would you like to come along?"

Boone let go of the bird's toy. "Me? Go to Stephanie's ballet?"

"If you're not interested, that's okay. I just thought I'd ask." She should have known better than to ask a jock to accompany her to a children's ballet recital.

"I'm interested," he quickly asserted. "It's just that Stephanie seems a bit out of sorts with me. I don't know if she'd want me there."

"Don't mind Stephanie. She's just gearing up for her teenage rebellion."

"Then I'll be there with bells on."

He smiled, and the simple gesture warmed Nixie to her toes.

If she'd had even the slightest inkling that their kiss beside the car had meant something to Boone, that thought was thoroughly dispelled the next week when he showed up with three more "applications."

This time she didn't leave the room, but stayed and acted interested in seeing who wanted to court her. If Boone could kiss and forget, then she would, too. Or, at least, pretend to.

"Change your mind about meeting someone through a personals ad?" Boone asked as she sat on the couch beside him. Chad was perched on his knee, and Stephanie sat close enough to scan the letters over his shoulder as he read them aloud.

"Curious," she responded, "just like you and the kids."

He gave her a sidelong look that let her know quite clearly he was suspicious of her change in attitude.

"Come on," Stephanie urged. "Read."

"Yeah," Nixie prompted. "The man of my dreams could be in one of those letters."

When he took his time opening the first envelope, Nixie snatched the small bundle from his hand. "We don't have all year. I'm not getting any younger, you know." She grinned to see the surprised look on his face. "If I'm going to meet these guys, I want to do it before I'm an old maid."

She cleared her throat and began reading the first letter. It rambled at length about his career and hobbies. Not exciting, but not a turnoff, either. It ended, "I'm a firm believer in marriage. My sixth wife left me last month, and I want to try again."

"Well," Boone piped up, "he certainly has plenty of experience for the job."

"Experience at being a husband," Stephanie said. "But does he have experience at being a daddy?"

Chad grabbed the letter and balled it up, mimicking Boone's action from the last time. "I vote no on this one."

Thank goodness! Nixie had been half afraid her son would overlook the man's failure at marriage in favor of his interest in car racing.

The next two were no better. One said he thought animals were great, but since he was highly allergic they would have to stay outside. That was enough to dissuade the children from considering him a possibility.

The last one wanted to know Nixie's career and income level. He had accrued some debts and reasoned the best way to pay them off would be to add another paycheck—Nixie's.

Nixie carried the letters to the trash can and dropped them in. She'd been relieved that all the letter writers seemed to have obvious flaws. Even though she'd pretended an interest in learning about the candidates, she would have had a hard time explaining to her children why she wouldn't want to meet a stranger who happened to fit their qualifications.

Coming back to the den, she reminded her family that this was the reason she'd been against the idea of the ad in the first place. "Anyone who's good enough to be your daddy is probably already taken," she added. "Now let's go. Uncle Jim and Aunt Laura are going to meet us at the restaurant before the recital. We'd best not keep them waiting."

As it turned out, Boone, Nixie and the children had to wait for Uncle Jim and Aunt Laura. Boone made the waitress giggle when he asked for a child's placemat for himself, then colored the cartoon characters and worked the math puzzles with the children. They seemed to enjoy having him join their fun, and Nixie was pleased to see that Stephanie had dropped her sullen attitude. Nixie was glad she'd talked her daughter into wearing the ballet-slipper necklace Boone had given her. He'd noticed it right away and commented how it couldn't do justice to her own sparkling beauty.

The Thomases had come to this restaurant before, but with Boone here, their group now seemed complete. It would have been like this if Paul had lived, Nixie thought.

With a small shake of her head, she realized it wouldn't have been the same. Paul had stayed so busy with work, he had seldom made time for family outings. She wondered if they would still be married now. Would the tiny hill of dissension his workaholism had created in their marriage have eventually grown into a mountain too tall for either to overcome?

She looked across the table at Boone, sitting hunched over the paper placemat. His every move was being copied by Chad. He must have noticed it, too, for he stuck his tongue out one side of his mouth as if in concentration. Chad copied that. When Boone picked up his glass of soda and took a sip, Chad reached for his milk, and stopped.

"Milk is sissified," he told Boone. "Mind if I have some of yours?"

"Sure," Boone told him, passing the glass. "Just don't get any backwash in my drink..."

Chad grinned and put the glass to his lips.

"...because I don't want it mixing with *my* backwash."

The boy sputtered, and lemon-lime soda went down the front of his shirt.

"Psyched you out," Boone said, handing him his napkin.

Nixie and Stephanie handed over their napkins, as well. They shared a look that only mothers and daughters understand. Nixie looked up to find Boone watching them.

"What?" he asked. "At least we weren't playing grossout."

Stephanie giggled. "Last time we played that, Mom sent us to our rooms. She said it's dangerous to laugh while you're eating because you could choke. Right, Mom?"

Before Nixie could answer, Uncle Jim and Aunt Laura joined them, filling the remaining two seats at the table.

As the waitress took the food orders for all of them, Nixie was surprised to see Stephanie take off the satin-slipper necklace and tuck it into her purse.

What was worse, Boone had seen it, too.

Chapter Six

The evening went downhill after that.

When the waitress had asked Chad if he wanted his chopped steak cooked medium like his father's, Stephanie had loudly corrected her, saying their father was in heaven. Chad, on the other hand, had reveled in the mistake.

Then Stephanie had clung to her uncle's hand and made it clear she wanted nothing to do with Boone. It got so bad that when Nixie went backstage with her later to help with her costume, she gave her daughter a firm chewing-out. She doubted that the talk did any good.

Nixie couldn't understand why Stephanie, who was normally so pleasant and cheerful with everyone, would so openly reject Boone.

When Boone drove them home after the recital, Chad wouldn't stop chattering and trying to monopolize his new mentor's attention. Nixie worried that her son had an enormous case of hero worship. What would happen when he found out that Boone, like all men, had his own shortcomings?

Goodness, Nixie thought, it would be so much easier if both children would react the same. Then she'd only have to find one solution rather than two.

"I apologize for Stephanie's behavior," Nixie told Boone after her daughter had unceremoniously dumped the beautiful long-stemmed red rose he'd given her onto the couch and run into the kitchen to put her other rose—the pink one Uncle Jim had given her—into water. "I don't know what's gotten into her. She's never acted this way before."

"Don't apologize," Boone said, giving her a one-armed hug. "All these years it's been a tradition to have her family watch her perform. It must have felt weird to have an outsider tagging along."

Nixie shook her head. "I just don't understand it. She was fine in the beginning. Then something happened, and she changed from Dr. Jekyll into Mr. Hyde. If this is what she's like at eleven, I'm not looking forward to sixteen."

Boone smiled and took her hands in both of his. The simple gesture was comforting, and he seemed so full of understanding. This was one of those times when Nixie yearned for a partner to share the bad times with her, as well as the good. On days such as this, she envied the married women who had their husbands to share the burden of raising their children properly. As it was now, she could only hope she was doing the right thing.

"If she turns out just half as well as you did, she'll be one lucky lady," Boone said.

Chad came bounding down the steps wearing an oversize T-shirt that served as his sleepwear. "I'll see you

Wednesday for den meeting," he said, giving his Scout leader a high-five.

"Sure thing, pal." Boone turned loose of Nixie's hand and took a couple of playful punches at the boy. "Before I forget it again, why don't you run and get my Scout pin?"

The look Chad gave him was one Nixie was well familiar with. He'd worn it the time he made a fake volcano and got baking soda all over the living room. He'd given her that look when she'd been looking for the gauze to bandage a scrape on Stephanie's arm and he told her he'd used it all to dress up as a mummy. And he'd used the same expression when his teacher had called to tell her Chad had completed his homework assignment of learning five new words and their definitions from the dictionary but that they'd all been naughty words.

The look was one of guilt. Nixie's heart lurched. She hadn't thought the evening could get any worse, and now she was being proven wrong.

"Did you break Boone's pin?" she demanded.

He shook his head. "I can't find it," he whispered.

Although the boy frequently got into mischief, he was always truthful about his misdeeds. Now, however, he seemed different, subdued even. Nixie couldn't help wondering what else was going on that he wasn't telling.

"I don't know where it is," he mumbled.

"Then I suggest you go upstairs and find it." Nixie turned him around and gave him a little push.

"Don't be too hard on him," said Boone. "It'll turn up."

She wondered whether to voice her fears to Boone, then decided he might be able to help her deal with Chad if she was able to point out the problem. Then again, he might just laugh away her concern and suggest she was overreacting as she had the night she'd gone back to the camporee. She took the plunge on the off chance he might be able to help her deal with the problem.

"I think it's wonderful how Chad looks up to you. It was cute how he kept copying you this evening," she began. Boone's answering smile was quick. "But I'm worried that he might be obsessed with the idea of being just like you. It seems like he's carrying this mentor thing too far."

Boone's proud smile turned to a scowl. "What's your point?"

Nixie swallowed. The last thing she wanted to do was hurt his feelings, especially after all he'd done for Chad's confidence. And she didn't want to heap another insult on top of those thrown by Stephanie this evening.

"You've been a terrific influence on Chad. The teacher said he'd settled down at school and is less disruptive, and he doesn't tease Stephanie as much as he used to."

"But?"

Nixie turned away from him as she thought about how to phrase what she had to say. "I'm worried that Chad is developing an unhealthy attachment to you." She turned to face him and saw that his features were rigidly composed. "He's so obsessed with emulating you, I suspect he may have taken the pin because he wants so much to be like you."

"Has he ever stolen anything before?"

"No, but—"

"Then it seems you may be jumping to conclusions."

He was angry, and Nixie had only meant to solicit his help. She'd really managed to stick her foot in it this time. "I've seen that look of his before. I know when he's hiding something."

"Then why didn't you ask him instead of accusing him?"

"Because," Nixie blurted, pushing her hair behind her shoulder, "I made the mistake of thinking you might be able to help me handle the situation."

A cat yowled upstairs. A moment later, Stephanie came thumping down the steps with Stormy in her arms. She ran past them, went through the kitchen to the utility room, and locked the little creature in.

"It's not going to work, Mom," she declared as she stormed back into the room. She shot a guarded look at Boone before continuing. "Precious doesn't want anyone else in our family. Everything was just fine before the new guy showed up."

Tears threatened to spill from her eyes.

Nixie opened her arms and held Stephanie to her. The child's dark blond hair fell against Nixie's shoulders. She would be tall, like her father, Nixie thought inanely.

Strange how she'd been thinking of Paul more, lately. She wondered if it had anything to do with Boone's presence in their lives. At the oddest times, she found herself comparing Boone to her late husband.

She looked up to see Boone backing away.

"I guess I'd better go now. Let me know if you want me to find Stormy another home."

Nixie hated to see him go home on this sour note. She wanted to apologize for the rotten evening. She wanted to thank him for being a good sport. She wanted to walk outside with him and kiss him good night. Instead all she said was, "Thanks, I'll let you know."

He gave Stephanie's hair a light tug, then hollered up the stairs to Chad. "Be ready for den meeting on Wednesday. And keep looking for that pin."

It seemed as though the minute he was gone, Stephanie's tears dried.

"Don't worry about Stormy," Nixie told her daughter. "I'm sure he'll find a welcome place in our family before long."

Stephanie scowled. "I wouldn't count on it."

When Boone arrived Wednesday evening, Tarzan was screeching at the top of his lungs. The sound effects were enough to rival any Amazon jungle movie.

"What's the matter with him?" Boone yelled over the din. He approached the cage with a finger in each ear and stared curiously at the noisy beast.

"He's mad because Chad won't take him out of the cage," Nixie said.

"Aw, Chad, let the little guy out," Boone urged.

"But, Boone, he'll plop on my Scout shirt."

Nixie watched as Boone released the bird-proof latch and let the loudmouth out of his cage. Tarzan moved from his finger and sidestepped up his forearm. He lifted his scaly feet high as if the hair on Boone's arm tickled them, then he bent over and teased one of the hairs with his beak.

"He's not used to furry arms," Chad said when Boone chuckled.

Boone leaned over and whispered something to Chad. When her son's face clouded and he shook his head in the negative, Nixie knew Boone had asked about the pin. They had turned Chad's room upside down looking for the memento, but had been unsuccessful in the search.

Just as she'd suspected they would.

"I'll go look one more time," the boy said, and dashed upstairs.

Stephanie was in the kitchen loading the dishwasher. Nixie had been surprised when she'd volunteered to handle the job just as she heard Boone's car pull up in the driveway.

"Excuse me a moment," Nixie told Boone. "I have to get some money to cover Chad's Scout dues." She left him talking to the bird.

When she came back, he was still talking to the feathered mimic in a hushed tone.

"If you talk quietly when you're teaching him a word, he'll only repeat it in a whisper," she mentioned.

"What makes you think we're not having a conversation?" he asked. "Tarzan's been telling me his recent discoveries about how to achieve increased aerodynamics."

"Don't let him fool you," Nixie warned with a teasing grin. "Tarzan's just repeating what he and Chad discussed last night. That bird doesn't have an original thought in his head."

The smile he gave Nixie stirred her in a way she couldn't remember ever feeling before. It was a smile of appreciation and humor that made Nixie feel as if she'd just made the wittiest remark in the world. It made her feel brilliant, unique and . . . special.

She gazed back at the man who made her feel this way. What was it about him that turned her emotions upside down? In high school he'd caused her blood pressure to rise with his relentless heckling. And now he was giving her heart palpitations with a mere look. If she wasn't careful around Boone Shelton, she might be one of the next rescue victims for her squad. She just hoped it wouldn't be because of a broken heart.

Boone was the first to break the soft silence that had grown between them. "Your kids are going to think they've hit the jackpot today.'' He patted the papers in his shirt pocket. ''They received an all-time high of four applications to choose from.''

Nixie's jaw went slack, and she firmly clamped it shut. She felt so off-balance she reached for the wall to steady herself. A minute ago he'd been making eyes at her that said, in no uncertain language, he had tender feelings for her.

Could they have been the kind of tender feelings someone has for a friend? Her mind raced. No. That kiss they'd shared the night of the camporee assured her otherwise.

Chad returned from his room, giving Nixie a moment to gather her jumbled thoughts. He shrugged at Boone, his lips pressed into a thin line.

''Don't worry,'' Boone told him. ''You'll find it soon. Just keep looking.''

Nixie came back to reality with a snap. She supposed it was possible Chad had lost the treasured Scout pin. But he swore he hadn't left his bedroom with it, and the three of them had hunted in, around, and under everything in his room. Maybe it would turn up soon. She hoped so, even if it meant proving Boone right. Knowing Boone as she did, she wouldn't put him above an ''I told you so.''

He handed the envelopes to Chad, who immediately called his sister into the room.

As they once again settled themselves onto the sofa to peruse the letters, Nixie felt an ache in the pit of her being. She had thought there might be something special between them, but here he was, excitedly screening daddy candidates with her children. She couldn't bring herself to join them as she had done last time, but some morbid sense of curiosity forced her to stay.

She flopped down into the chair beside Tarzan's cage and picked up a magazine. Flipping through it, she found a list of "Ten Sure Signs That Your Man Is Right For You." Maybe she should give it to the children to use as a checklist.

Boone sat with a child to either side of him. He was crazy about these kids and wished he could apply for the job they'd advertised. But he'd already caused enough problems for them. Although he didn't like to think it was so, there was a slight possibility that Nixie was right about Chad going overboard trying to imitate him. And then there was Stephanie who, for whatever reason, had decided she wanted nothing to do with him.

He glanced up at Nixie. It was obvious she was pretending to read that magazine. He couldn't blame her for sitting on the other side of the room, away from him. Not after his high school reaction to the feelings that had passed between them. Why hadn't he simply told her she was beautiful instead of bringing up the latest batch of applicants?

Boone ripped open the first envelope. He hadn't told her she was beautiful, he reminded himself, because it was hard to say that kind of thing when the mere thought paralyzes your lips and squeezes your lungs until you can't breathe.

He took a deep breath and read the first one out loud. It was a well-composed, thoughtful letter that portrayed the sender as an intelligent, caring person. "Hey, you can't beat this one," he told the children. "This guy even put a couple of Bible verses at the bottom of the letter. Proverbs 13:24 and Ephesians 5:23."

Nixie looked up. Boone just smiled at her as Chad raced Stephanie to the bookshelf to get the Bible.

Stephanie found the first verse and read it. "'He that spareth his rod hateth his son: but he that loveth him chasteneth him betimes.'"

"What does that mean?" Chad asked.

Boone smiled again. "It means this applicant is in favor of corporal punishment."

The boy's eyes grew large, and he put his hands in back of him as if to protect his rear. "Nobody's going to punish my corporal!"

"Let's see what the other verse is," Boone urged.

Stephanie read again, her voice strong and clear. "'Ephesians 5:23. For the husband is the head of the wife, even as—'"

"I vote no on this one," Nixie interjected.

"Then it's unanimous." Stephanie ripped the letter into small pieces and placed them on the sofa beside her.

Like a tiny green hawk, Tarzan swooped down on the paper bits, nabbed one, and carried it back to his cage.

Boone chuckled as he sneaked a peek at the next letter. "If you didn't like the last one," he told Nixie, "then you probably won't like this one, either."

She looked up from watching the bird play with the paper. "Let me guess. He's a man of the nineties. The eighteen-nineties."

"You got it! This guy says he believes most women today are too uppity and don't know their place. He wants someone whose only career would be keeping his house clean and cooking his meals."

In answer, Nixie shook open the magazine and put it in front of her face.

"Since you didn't like that one," Boone persisted, "maybe you'd like *this* guy's sense of adventure." The magazine came down a few inches until Nixie's eyes showed above it. "He's moving to Alaska soon and doesn't want to go alone."

"No," Chad insisted. "Tarzan's a jungle bird. He wouldn't like it there."

The magazine went back up.

Boone chuckled again, and Nixie could feel her face burning. As she recalled, they had gone through three letters so far. That meant there was one more, and then Boone would leave for the den meeting. Trying to take her mind off Boone and what he was doing, she tried to focus on the words in front of her. That was when she realized why Boone had laughed just now. She rotated the magazine until it was right side up.

"Nixie, darlin'." The masculine voice was deep and smooth, and full of innuendo.

She put the magazine down again, and found him staring at her, his eyes full of unspoken promises . . . and maybe a little bit of mischief.

"What's the maximum number of kids you want?"

The way he said it made it seem as if he were offering to give them to her. Nixie licked her lips. "Uh, three or four, I guess."

As soon as she answered him, she wondered if she were setting herself up to be the target of another one of his jokes.

In an effort to cover her tracks, she added, "But two are plenty. We have lots of love to go around, don't we?" she urged the children.

Boone handed the final envelope to Stephanie. "Then you may as well toss this one, too. He has five children of his own and wants to know if you two are old enough to help watch his young ones."

"I'm almost old enough to baby-sit," Stephanie replied, "but I don't want to do it for free."

Nixie gave a small sigh of relief. Although the children had received many more replies from the advertisement than she'd ever expected, none had panned out. She was glad she hadn't been put in the awkward position of refusing to go out with any strange men.

A movement near the cage caught her eye. Tarzan was busily tucking bits of paper under the cloth beneath his cage. Nixie looked closer. From the size of the lumps, she guessed he'd been stashing more than paper.

She reached over and lifted a corner of the cloth. Tarzan shrieked and snatched the sunflower seed that had been hidden in the folds.

Next she found a chunk of withered carrot. Cupping her hand, she started collecting the treasures. A peanut, a paper clip, Stephanie's hair barrette . . .

Tarzan cocked his head and watched as she stood and proceeded to the other side of the cage.

Precious walked through the room, diverting Tarzan's attention for a moment. He gave a full-volume bark and then laughed maniacally when the yellow cat shot past into the next room.

A red building block, Nixie's gold shoulder-duster earring, the plastic ball with the bell inside that Stephanie had insisted she buy for Precious . . .

"What are you doing?" Chad asked.

"Going on a treasure hunt." She handed Stephanie the key to her diary, gave Chad the small toy car she'd found, and returned a miniature wooden apple to its rightful place in the decorative basket atop the television. "Your bird is a kleptomaniac."

Feeling three pairs of eyes upon her, Nixie turned to face them. Their expressions told her they had the same idea. In another moment, they were all searching the folds of fabric beneath Tarzan's cage.

"I found a quarter," exclaimed Stephanie. "Finders, keepers."

Chad held something between his thumb and forefinger. "E-ew, and I found a bobby pin."

Suddenly, Boone's searching hands stopped as he uncovered the object of their attention. Slowly, as if he were a prospector who had just discovered gold, he lifted it for all to see. Other than a slight curve in the metal post, the pin appeared to be undamaged.

Nixie's eyes left the cherished Cub Scout pin and met his blue gaze. There was no "I told you so" in his expression, just relief. Nixie, on the other hand, was gripped with guilt. How could she have suspected her son of taking the pin? Ever since Boone had come back into her life, she hadn't been thinking straight. Why else would she suspect Chad of behavior that was so out of character for him?

Why was her world so topsy-turvy lately? Even her sleep was often disrupted with images of clear blue eyes and shaggy blond hair. And in her waking hours those same blue eyes were turning her insides to mush.

After straightening the metal post that Tarzan had obviously bent with his strong, hooked beak, Boone turned to Chad and secured the pin above the boy's pocket.

"You were due to receive this at tonight's den meeting but, considering the circumstances, I'm going to present it to you now." He solemnly shook Chad's hand. "Congratulations on making such progress with the projects in your Cub Scout manual."

Nixie smiled with pride at her young man. Quickly she hugged Chad before he could resist the "icky" show of affection.

Turning her attention back to Boone, she said, "Thank you for your understanding." She wanted to say more, but what else was there? Thanks for believing in my son when I didn't?

Chad fingered the pin that had grown dull over time. "Awesome, man! Thanks."

Boone squeezed the boy's shoulder. "Looks like you have cause to celebrate, my man. When I earned that pin, my mother drove my sister and me over to Blowing Rock, and we spent the day at Tweetsie Railroad. We could make it a tradition and take you there on Saturday."

Chad turned to Nixie. "Yeah, and when my son earns his first Scout pin, I can take *him*. Right, Mom?"

It seemed that with every turn, Boone was becoming more firmly wedged into her life. But there was no way she could deny her son, especially after her brief lack of faith in him. "Sure, honey."

As Boone got out of the car to fill it up with gas, he tossed his wallet to Chad in the back seat. "Here, pal. Dig out a twenty for me, will you?"

Nixie watched from the front seat as Chad poked around for the bill. He seemed proud to have been chosen for the task, and Nixie instinctively knew it was Boone's way of showing his trust in the boy. He wanted Chad to know he had complete faith in him, and he was giving him an opportunity to prove his trustworthiness.

It was times such as these that made Nixie feel overwhelmed by the responsibility of being both mother and father to her children.

Chad handed Boone the twenty and continued to look through the wallet. He looked up and caught Nixie watching him. "I'm just looking at the pictures."

When Boone returned, Chad asked, "Who is this pretty lady with the blond hair?"

Nixie felt herself stiffen. He'd always been partial to blondes in high school. She didn't want to hear about his conquests, past or present. "Chad, maybe you should give Boone his billfold back."

"That's okay." Boone pulled out into traffic, and eased back in his seat. "It's my sister, Ellen," he told Chad. "I think she's pretty, too."

"Oh," he said. "Then I guess this old lady is your mother?"

"Chad!"

Boone reached over and patted her hand. "No problem, Nix. I'm sure anyone over fifty seems old to a kid Chad's age."

Her son flipped past to the next photo. "Hey, where'd you get a picture of Mom?"

Stephanie, who'd been silent until now, leaned closer to her brother. "Let me see that." She studied it for a moment, then looked at Nixie. "I didn't know you ever looked so glamorous."

Nixie took the wallet that her daughter handed her. The face that stared back from behind the clear plastic protector did, indeed, look incredibly like her.

The shoulder-length auburn tresses were curled and skillfully arranged around the small heart-shaped face. The artfully applied makeup accentuated the wide-apart brown eyes, high cheekbones and full lips.

It was almost like looking into a mirror, except the woman staring back at her had a more worldly appearance. There was a hard edge about her that made it seem as though she would take no guff from anyone.

Boone cleared his throat. "Uh, I thought I'd taken that one out. It's Cheryl, my ex-wife."

Chapter Seven

The sights, the rides and the food they bought from the vendors at the amusement park should have been enough to distract Nixie's mind from the image of the woman in the photo. But they didn't.

Instead, for the entire morning she felt like a zombie going through the motions of enjoying their day at Tweetsie Railroad.

During the magic show at the outdoor theater, Nixie wondered if Boone had noticed the similarity when he first met Cheryl. On the ferris wheel she told herself she was being ridiculous—after all, hadn't she herself married someone whose features vaguely resembled Boone's? On the twirling swings, she mentally argued that their spouses' looks had nothing to do with the reason she and Boone had married them. And as they dressed in period costumes and posed for pictures, she remembered that one of the reasons she'd been attracted to Paul was because of his gentle teasing.

Later, when they bought cotton candy, Nixie wondered if Cheryl liked the messy confection. The woman in the photo didn't look the type, she decided. Nixie tore off a hank of the pink candy, popped it into her mouth, and licked the stickiness off her thumb. Nixie also felt certain Cheryl didn't look like the type for whom smiles came easily. And if that were the case, it was no wonder their marriage didn't last. How could it, when she had been teamed with a joker like Boone?

She strolled with Boone and the children past a small cemetery that was fenced off from the rest of the park. At first she thought the tiny fence-enclosed area was for show, perhaps part of a setting for a Wild West skit. On closer inspection, she realized the gravestones were real and the dates were of this century. The theme park must have sprung up around the cemetery, she guessed.

Boone was leaning against the fence, pointing to the large stone closest to them and telling the children his mother's side of the family was related to the Greenes buried here. "We're also distantly related to the Enzers in Boone, North Carolina," he added.

"Is that where you got your name?" asked Chad.

"Sure is. My parents had only been married about six months when I was born, and my mother was very homesick."

Stephanie pulled the last of the cotton candy from her paper cone. "But it takes about nine..." She blushed. "Oh, never mind."

Boone gave her ponytail a gentle tug. "That's right," he said without embarrassment. "She and my father were too young for that kind of commitment. That's why their marriage didn't last."

Nixie stood quietly beside him. He had easily shared a part of his life that many would have preferred to keep private. But, without lecturing, he'd used the information to drive home a valuable lesson to the children.

"Anyway, my mother missed Boone—the county—so much she named me after it."

Nixie couldn't resist. "Aren't you glad she wasn't from Charlotte?"

Boone whirled around, raised his hands in monster-like fashion, and came after her. Nixie took off up the hill toward the train platform, two squealing children behind her, and Boone in hot pursuit.

They didn't slow down until they reached the platform. Nixie was breathless as she slid into the seat directly in front of the one her children had chosen. Boone scooted in beside her and grabbed her in a bear hug as they waited for the rest of the passengers to board.

Laughing, Nixie leaned into him. It was a good feeling. As they caught their breaths, she relaxed against the hard, warm wall of his chest. Leaning her head against his shoulder, she giggled and whispered, "Or Kitty Hawk?"

He clawed his free hand above her. The laughing sparkle in his eyes let her know he was enjoying this game. "I'm warning you...."

More than a little curious what "punishment" he had in store for her, Nixie giggled again. "Or Faith?"

Making like a vampire, Boone bent over her and pretended to bite her upper arm.

The sensation sent little goose bumps down Nixie's spine. "Sophia?"

He playfully attacked the round of her shoulder. "Hush!" he said in a feigned accent, 'or I vill make you pay zee ultimate price."

Next time he was sure to go for her neck. The lure was too great. "Sapphire!"

As soon as his lips touched her neck, Nixie melted like ice cream on a warm day. She was breathless once again, this time from giddy laughter and the sensations Boone stirred merely by breathing against her skin.

Chad popped over the back of their seat and peered down at them. "How about Bald Head Island?"

Nixie looked up to see Stephanie's head appear beside her brother's. "Or *Turkey*, North Carolina!" the girl goaded.

Pulling away from Nixie, Boone growled and lunged for the children, which sent them into fits of giggling.

Nixie sat up straighter and set about composing herself. She watched, amused, as Boone reached over the back of their seat and made wild grabbing motions with his hand.

The movement of the train, as it started, aborted their frenzied play. Boone settled down beside her, and hung his arm over her shoulder. He turned toward her and lightly dropped a kiss on her forehead.

"E-ew, barf-o-rama," she heard Chad mutter behind them.

It had been a long time since she had laughed so freely. For the past eight years, Nixie had been working so hard making sure her family was healthy and happy that she hadn't found the time or energy to let loose like this.

Too late, she wondered what the other passengers must think of their enthusiastic display. Glancing past Boone to the couple seated across from them, she saw a wistful smile on the older woman's face. Her husband gazed lovingly down at her and took her hand in his. It was clear they were remembering with fondness similar episodes from their own past.

Nixie turned her gaze back to Boone's rugged visage. He was so big and rough-looking that he hardly seemed the type to be cavorting so childishly with her and the kids.

Her thoughts took her back to the older couple. They had obviously spent many happy years together. What, she wondered, did her own future hold for her? Would she have someone special to share a history with? Would it be someone who would make her laugh and keep her from taking life's daily grind too seriously?

Goodness, she hoped so.

Would it be Boone?

She sighed softly. Experience had taught her she shouldn't take him too seriously, either...no matter how delightfully giddy his touch made her feel.

Besides, he was determined to set her up with some stranger who had nothing better to do than answer personals ads in the newspaper, she thought bitterly.

The train rounded a curve as they made their way through the wooded "frontier" land. The motion gently urged her closer to Boone, and she didn't resist the pull.

It might hurt later, but she couldn't worry about that now. For now, it was too pleasant enjoying his laughter and the closeness of his powerful body next to hers.

They were laughing as they left Tweetsie Railroad and climbed into the sun-heated car. The stifling humidity didn't seem to affect the children's enthusiasm. They recounted the day's adventures while waiting for the air conditioner to cool the interior of the car.

"How about when those Indians stopped the train at the pioneer settlement?" said Stephanie. "I thought I would die laughing when Mom asked that young brave if the medicine man put those braces on his teeth."

Boone snickered as he buckled his seat belt. "It did sort of ruin the effect."

Nixie lounged back in her seat and crossed her arms in front of her. "Are you saying you bought the blond hair and freckles on that brave?"

He grinned back at her. "Actually, it was the sneakers that clued me in."

"I liked the bird show best," Chad chimed in. "It sure would be great to have a blue and gold macaw like the one that rode the little bicycle."

Boone reached back and patted the boy on the knee. "Sometimes people wish for things they don't have when all they have to do is look in their own backyard."

"If you're talking about Tarzan, we don't let him go outside."

"It's a figure of speech," said Boone. He switched to the passing lane, then picked up where he'd left off. "If you ask me, your bird's much smarter than that macaw. You're just so used to having Tarzan around that you're not aware of how special he is."

"Maybe."

"The same could be said about your search for a daddy," he added significantly.

Startled, Nixie looked up from the stuffed toy turtle she held in her lap.

He gave her a saucy wink. "Could be there's someone you already know who would make a fine daddy."

Nixie touched his arm, silently pleading with him not to raise Chad's hopes. Or hers. "Boone, it's one thing to tease me, but please don't involve the children in your jokes."

"Who said I was joking?"

"Hey, I know!" exclaimed Chad as if an idea had just occurred to him. "What about *you!* You already have experience with kids from being the den leader. And you'd suit Mom because you must read a lot if you own the newspaper. Right, Mom?''

"That's a stupid idea if I ever heard one," Stephanie butted in.

"It is not!" Chad leaned forward in his seat. "Is he good-looking enough for you, Mom?"

Boone sat up straight behind the steering wheel, batting his eyelashes, flashing his best smile.

What could she do? If she agreed, it would lend encouragement to an unwise pairing. But if she said no to discourage her son, she'd be lying.

Boone had said he wasn't joking. Did he truly think something besides arguing and teasing could come of a relationship between them? Although it first seemed preposterous to her, the idea actually held appeal for Nixie. After all, as much as she tried to deny it, she had come to look forward to his frequent visits. In fact, she'd been afraid he would run out of reasons to come see them, so she had come up with an idea for a rescue squad fund-raiser that would ensure further contact with Boone. She just hadn't told him yet about the upcoming donkey baseball game between the emergency services volunteers and Lakewood businessmen.

She looked again at the man who had wedged himself so firmly into her life. The wispy blond hair that reminded her so much of her son's fell in disarray across his forehead. The smiling eyes were so full of humor it was a wonder there was room left over for all that incredible blue. His face, like the man behind it, was strong, straight, and full of character. As Nixie focused on the rows of even, white teeth, she wondered how they'd survived his rough-and-tumble days on the football field. And his lips, narrow and firm, tempted her with memories of their first kiss the night of the camporee. Oh, what wonderful reassurance he had given her.

Her eyes met his, and she realized they held more than humor. They held compassion, concern and caring. For the first time, Nixie admitted to herself that their kiss had less to do with reassurance than with their feelings for each other.

He was still waiting for her answer. Was he good-looking enough?

"Well, Chad," she began, "when you're choosing a daddy, looks are a lot less important than a person's values and whether he's compatible with the rest of the family."

"Yeah, I forgot about that. You don't believe in corporal punishment, do you?" he asked Boone.

Boone grinned. "For someone like you? I think you're bright enough to reason with. Besides, I plan to build you up on my weight machines. I wouldn't want you getting even with me after you're big enough to punch me out."

"Chad, we need to talk," Stephanie declared.

For the rest of the ride home, they whispered furiously in the back seat. It was obvious Stephanie was against the idea of including Boone's name among their list of candidates.

Nixie switched on the radio in the hope that it would cover their remarks. It wouldn't do to have her children unwittingly insult Boone after he'd been kind enough to treat them to a day at Tweetsie Railroad.

"How about that?" Boone said. "The answer was right there in front of us all along. Isn't it amazing we didn't see it before?"

"I think we need to talk, too." She had to know where he stood on this before he got Chad's hopes up any further—or upset Stephanie unnecessarily. As for Nixie, she couldn't bear it if this was another one of his impractical jokes.

Uncle Jim and Aunt Laura had graciously agreed to let the children eat dinner with them so Nixie and Boone could have some time alone. Boone had opened the door on a possibility that Nixie knew neither should be too quick to act upon.

Of course, the children didn't get out the door without Stephanie breaking into tears first. After Chad had told Boone some of the tricks his uncle had played on the family, Boone had suggested Chad remove the batteries from Jim's remote control when he wasn't looking.

At that, Stephanie had protested loudly, saying Chad was mean and disloyal to do such a thing to someone who loved them as much as Uncle Jim did. She seemed overly protective, and Nixie couldn't imagine why her normally mild-mannered daughter had become so explosive. She made a mental note to have a long talk with her tomorrow, after Stephanie had calmed down. Meanwhile, Aunt Laura and Uncle Jim could help distract her from whatever had been bothering her lately.

As Nixie assembled a wokful of chicken stir fry, Boone stayed in the living room, talking to the parrot. She supposed he needed to gather his thoughts, just as she did.

They ate in polite silence. What, Nixie wondered, did one say to a man who has invited himself to become a permanent member of their family?

Boone also seemed thoughtful. She frequently caught him watching her and discovered she liked being the focus of his attention.

While she carried the dishes to the dishwasher, Boone fed some of the vegetables to Tarzan. As she entered the living room, she found him talking quietly to the bird. It seemed he'd had more to say to Tarzan this evening than he had to her.

"We need to figure out where we stand on this daddy issue," said Nixie, "before anything else is said to the children."

Boone nodded his agreement. He tried to put Tarzan back in the cage, but when the bird refused, Boone gave up and let him perch on his shoulder. He followed Nixie to the couch and sat down beside her.

"You already know where I stand," he said. "I thought my suggestion to Chad was a good one. Now we just need to know how you feel about it."

Tarzan leaned forward as if trying to catch Nixie's response.

This was disconcerting enough. She didn't need two pairs of eyes watching her. Nixie folded her hands in her lap and studied them. Nibbling the inside of her cheek, she turned to face him. "In high school, you used to tease me a lot."

He squirmed, then gave her a faint smile. "Yeah, I did, didn't I?"

His reaction let Nixie know he wasn't proud of the torture he'd put her through. "How do I know you're not teasing me again?"

Tarzan lost interest and jumped off Boone's shoulder to climb the venetian blind cord.

Boone moved closer to Nixie, his very nearness affecting her like a powerful drug. His blue eyes bored a hole into her soul. "Will this prove how serious I am?"

His arms slid around her. In the next moment, his lips touched hers.

Nixie had replayed their first kiss over and over in her mind, trying to remember and savor the moment in all of its toe-tingling wonder. And now he was actually kissing her again. She felt like the luckiest woman in the world.

This was different from that first kiss. Not as raw and demanding. This time, it was tender and full of promise. That night at the car he'd stirred long-suppressed physical needs within her. Tonight, he touched Nixie's emotional needs.

Nixie had been on her share of dates, and she knew what a man wanted from a woman. But this man wanted her children, too, and that simple fact affected her libido more than any candlelight dinner or expensive champagne could ever do.

When he ended the kiss, he didn't pull away. He was close enough for her to feel his breath on her face. His hand touched hers, and he placed her palm against his chest. Even through the pullover shirt, Nixie could feel the thumpety-thump that surely matched her own heartbeat. His lips brushed hers as he spoke. "Believe me now?"

She smiled and slid her hand up to touch the blond tufts at the back of his neck. "I could use some more convincing."

He kissed her again, this time pushing her down onto the couch so that he sprawled beside her. His weight was braced on one elbow, and his left knee lay intimately across the top of Nixie's legs. Nixie was aware of the arousal that his jeans could not contain, and she liked knowing she was the cause of it.

"Oh, Nix, I've wanted to hold you like this for so long."

Nixie squirmed with pleasure, and it thrilled her to know the action excited him more. "So you're saying you want me for my body?"

"I want *you,* Nixie. I want you and everything that is a part of you. Chad and Stephanie. Precious and Stormy. Your aunt and uncle. Even this crazy bird that's walking on my back." He kissed her lightly and let his lips trail down to her neck, where he gave her a playful bite. "Do you suppose he'll tell anyone what we've been doing?"

"If you're going to be my children's daddy, what does it matter?"

It had slipped out so unexpectedly. Nixie hadn't consciously accepted the suggestion he'd made to Chad earlier today. It was an intuitive thing, something that had felt so right that she automatically knew it was the right thing to do.

She knew they cared for each other. Though neither had spoken the words, she knew those feelings were love. And she wanted Boone as much as he wanted her.

Boone squinted at the woman who was smiling up at him. If he didn't know better, he'd think she was turning the tables on him with a joke of her own. But he didn't need his glasses to read the expression on her face. It reflected his own feelings. Happiness, contentment . . . love.

He wondered how he could be so lucky. He wondered what he should say. The woman certainly had a way of catching him off guard.

Tarzan sauntered up Boone's shoulder and craned his feathered neck until he looked him straight in the eye. "Can you talk?" the bird asked.

Then, with a whirr of wings and a raucous laugh, the parrot took off for his cage.

"He's right," Boone said. "I'm speechless." His fingers trailed upward along her arm and made circles on her shoulder before blazing a path down her collarbone. She offered no resistance. He casually drew his fingers farther downward, between the twin hills of sumptuous flesh to the valley of her flat abdomen, then stopped at the inward curve of her waist. He drew her closer, pressing her to his body, tormenting himself further with the desire to have her as completely as a man can have a woman. "So your answer is yes? You'll let me be Stephanie's and Chad's daddy?"

She smiled and arched upward, the simple action making him want to rip the buttons from her shirt and have his way with her. He'd waited more than fifteen years for her. His patience was giving out.

"If that was a proposal," she murmured against his lips, "it's the strangest one I've ever heard."

From there on, instinct took over. Her shirt came off agonizingly slowly. He tried to restrain himself, but by the time he got to the last button, he gave a yank, and it flew in an arc across the den.

Boone gave thanks for small favors when he found that her lacy bra was held together by a simple fastener in the front. He pushed the tiny cups aside and savored the delicacies beneath. Insanely, he envied those cups as he covered both pink-tipped mounds with his hands.

His body screamed with a blissful agony. As he reached down to unfasten his jeans, he covered her bare breast with kisses. Tracing circles around the nipple with his tongue, he watched, amazed, as the tip hardened and stood erect. Glancing up, he saw that Nixie's eyes were glazed with passion. He made himself more comfortable, then his hand found the snap at the top of her jeans and deftly parted it.

Nixie squirmed again, this time in an effort to assist his frustratingly slow fingers. She was hot, and his casual slowness only served to stoke the flames even higher. She finished the zipper herself and reached for the hem of his shirt. Pushing the fabric up, she let her fingers explore the hard, rounded planes of his chest. Her hand dipped lower and, upon the sharp intake of his breath, she could feel the rippled washboard muscles of his abdomen. Her questing fingers trailed lower still, following the soft path of hair to—

The doorbell rang.

Nixie and Boone froze. Their gazes locked, and Nixie saw that he seemed as confused as she. When it rang a second time, they both jumped to action, straightening and rearranging their mussed clothes and hair.

Running her fingers through her hair one final time, Nixie answered the door on the third ring.

"What took you so long?" Chad groused.

Standing on the porch behind the children, Aunt Laura took in Nixie's rumpled appearance. When Boone came behind Nixie and laid a hand on her waist, she said, "Never mind that, Chad. Let's just get Stephanie inside so we can tend to her."

"Stephanie? What's the matter with Stephanie?" Turning to her daughter, Nixie saw immediately what the problem was. The exposed areas of the girl's face and arms were covered with raised, red welts.

Stephanie scratched her stomach, then reached down and rubbed her thigh. "I itch, Mama."

Nixie's heart nearly broke at the sight of the ugly hives that covered her daughter's body. The last time she'd had the stress-induced rash was after Paul died. Because Nixie herself had been struggling to cope with the loss of her husband, she'd been unable to comfort Stephanie as much as she'd wanted.

Now things were different. She was stronger and better able to cope. Nixie resolved to find and remove the source of Stephanie's stress. In the meanwhile, she would make her as comfortable as possible.

Nixie urged her family into the house. "Chad, go fill the bathtub with cool water. Boone and Aunt Laura, would you sit with her and discourage her from scratching while I get the antihistamine?"

"Want me to put ice in the water?" Chad asked.

"No. Just make it slightly cooler than room temperature."

When she came back, Aunt Laura had her arm around the girl and Boone was patting Stephanie's hand in an effort to distract her from clawing the rash.

"Here," Nixie said, pouring the medicine into a spoon, "this should relieve the itching and swelling." She waited for Stephanie to swallow. With a silent wish, she hoped the rash came from an allergy rather than stress. Allergens were easier to avoid and simpler to fix than mental stress. "Did you eat or touch something that might have set this off?"

"Nothing out of the ordinary."

Stephanie scratched her neck, and Boone reached up to pull her hand away.

The water stopped flowing in the bathroom, and Chad returned a moment later. "We were just sitting around talking about what we did today. And I told 'em Boone might be our new daddy if you liked him enough."

"That's when the itching started," Aunt Laura interjected.

Stephanie glared at her brother. "You had no business saying that. Especially not to—"

"But it's true! Isn't it, Mom?"

Nixie winced as she noticed Stephanie digging furiously at a bright red welt under her arm. "Never mind that now. Stephanie needs to get in the tub."

She led her daughter to the bathroom and sprinkled baking soda in the bath water to help soothe the itching. While Stephanie soaked, Nixie went back to the den.

Boone stood as she entered the room. With a sinking heart, Nixie knew that he was the cause of her daughter's distress. But that didn't keep her from hoping there might be another reason for Stephanie's hives.

"I'll stay here tonight," Boone told her. Turning to Laura, he added, "On the couch, of course."

Aunt Laura nodded.

He took Nixie in his arms and gave her a gentle hug. "I'll stay up all night and look after her if she needs it. And if she's not better by morning, I'll drive her to the doctor."

For the briefest of moments, Nixie allowed herself to enjoy the feel of her cheek against his chest. She would love to have him spend the night, every night, and not on the couch, either. For now, though, she had to set aside her own wants and put Stephanie's needs first.

Reluctantly she broke the embrace. "That's very sweet of you. But I think it would be better if we kept things as normal as possible. She'll come around more quickly if there's less commotion in the house to upset her."

"And goodness knows she was upset this evening," said Aunt Laura. "I could tell she was agitated, but it really started showing after Chad fooled Jim by taking the batteries out of the remote control. And then when Chad started talking about you two getting married...well, you know what happened next."

Yes, Nixie knew what happened next. Her daughter had a stress reaction to the mere thought of her marrying Boone.

Maybe she'd be able to ease Stephanie's mind about Boone joining the family. But if she couldn't...

As much as she hated having to make the choice, her daughter's health would have to come before her own happiness.

Chapter Eight

After church the next day Aunt Laura caught Nixie slouched in the overstuffed chair beside Tarzan's cage and reading a romance novel. "Reading more of those love books?" she asked. "Don't you know it's more exciting to participate?" She gave Nixie an impish wink.

Nixie closed the historical saga. "I guess I just needed a happy ending to lift my spirits."

"Stephanie still sick?"

"No, she's mostly recovered. She doesn't itch unless she thinks about it."

Aunt Laura made herself at home on the couch. "Then what's on your mind?"

"I had a talk with her this morning. After some questioning, she admitted she doesn't want me to get involved with Boone."

"And it's too late for that, isn't it?"

Nixie gave an ironic laugh. "I think I've been emotionally involved with Boone since high school. I was just too blind to see it."

"But Stephanie sees it, and she's reluctant to share her mother with someone else."

Nixie frowned and rubbed her earlobe. "I don't think that's it. At first I suspected she didn't want anyone to take Paul's place, but if that were the case, she wouldn't have bought that help wanted ad for a daddy."

Aunt Laura's sweet face was full of compassion. She was more than just her aunt, Nixie knew, she was her friend. And Nixie was grateful to have such a kind and caring friend.

"Don't worry, Nixie. It took you a while to get used to Boone, and you finally came around. Stephanie will come around, too."

"But that's where I'm confused. It's obvious she's crazy about him, yet she's working very hard to pretend she's not. It just doesn't make sense."

"Most kids don't make sense at that age. Give her time."

Stephanie called to them from upstairs. "Mom, you have company."

The front door burst open, and Chad came in, followed by Boone. "She's upstairs, and she looks normal again." With a wicked chuckle, Chad added in typical brotherly fashion, "Normal for *her.*"

Nixie stood to greet Boone. One look at that ruggedly handsome face, and she was wishing they were alone again. He smiled at her in a way that made her think he felt the same.

Chad buzzed around his hero like an annoying little gnat. Boone never broke eye contact with Nixie as he hefted the boy over his shoulder like a sack of potatoes.

"I was worried about Stephanie," Boone said. "Chad told me her rash is gone."

"Yes," she agreed. "Our home remedies seemed to do the trick." Nixie failed to add, however, that Stephanie's rash disappeared shortly after Boone had left. She hoped the cure had come from her home remedies rather than Boone's departure.

Aunt Laura stood and joined them. "Boone, we're going to the hospital this afternoon to see Nixie's new niece. Would you like to come along?"

By now Chad dangled upside down as Boone gripped his ankles and pretended to pound him into the floor. "I got a new cousin, Boone. Uncle Ryan and Aunt Francie weren't lucky enough to get a boy like me."

Shifting the boy's ankles to one hand, Boone held his other hand out at waist level and said to Nixie, "Little Ryan has a baby?"

Nixie nodded. "Isn't it amazing how fast kids grow up?" She wasn't referring to her little brother. If only she'd known how quickly she and Boone would grow up and go their separate ways, she may have taken notice of him in a different light. And their lives might have turned out vastly different.

But if that were the case, she wouldn't have had those years with Paul, nor would she have been blessed with these two wonderful children. What really mattered, she knew, was that even though it took them fifteen years to realize it, she and Boone were in love.

Suddenly she wanted more than anything to go to the maternity ward. She wanted to hear those tiny, high-pitched cries and share the joy of new life with Boone.

He turned his attention back to Chad. "Well, don't just hang there," he told the boy. "If you want to see your cousin, you'd better get a decent shirt on."

Later, at the hospital, they dawdled in front of the nursery window and stared at little Merrilee Cordaire. The baby had somehow freed one of her hands from the snug receiving blanket and sucked hungrily on her fist.

"You can tell she's a Cordaire," said Boone.

Nixie looked up at the man standing beside her. "How can you tell?"

"Look how pretty she is."

The look he gave Nixie told her he wasn't talking only about the Cordaire in the bassinet. Nixie took it as a personal compliment and, despite the fifteen years between her and the shy teenager she'd once been, she blushed.

"Gross," Chad said, clutching his stomach. "I'm going to get sick."

Stephanie grabbed her brother's hand and started pulling him in the direction Aunt Laura and Uncle Jim had gone moments before. "Let's go to Aunt Francie's room. After what she went through last night, I doubt she's in the mood to make goo-goo eyes at Uncle Ryan."

Nixie smiled as she watched her children walk hand-in-hand down the hospital corridor. Despite their frequent arguments and insults hurled at one another, they were best friends. They just wouldn't admit it. Maybe in a few more years they'd be mature enough to openly admit their affection for each other.

She looked up at Boone. He took her hand and swung it as the children had done when they sauntered away. She squeezed his hand, and he pulled her closer. Maybe that was what she and Boone had needed—time to mature. They'd been good friends all along, even amid the arguing and the teasing insults hurled at one another. Now they were old enough and mature enough to openly admit their affection for each other.

Boone pressed a kiss on her forehead, then rested his chin against her hair. "Next time we come to this ward, Nixie, I want it to be *our* baby in that bassinet. I was crazy to leave you that first time, and I won't let you get away again." The arm he had slung around her waist tightened with the intensity of his words. "I love you, Nixie. Marry me."

Nixie looked up into the face of the man who had been so many things to her. Adversary, ally, tormentor, friend, and now loved one. Now he was asking to be her husband and the father of her children. If it was only up to her she'd say yes without hesitation. But just as she did with all major family decisions, she wanted to discuss it with her children first. Her answer to Boone would affect their lives as well as her own.

"There was something in your newspaper's advice column recently that has stuck with me. She makes a lot of sense."

"You mean 'Ask Aunt Alice'?" Boone prompted.

"Yes. She told the person who'd written for advice that when people marry, they don't just join the one they've fallen in love with. They marry that person's family, as well. If you marry me, Boone, you marry my family. And I can't give you an answer without talking to my kids first."

He hugged her. "That's fair. But don't keep me waiting. I can't be patient much longer."

They walked hand-in-hand down the hospital corridor, swinging their arms in an echo of Stephanie's and Chad's action. As they approached Francie's room, they heard laughter.

When Nixie stepped inside, she was surprised to discover Stephanie was the only one not joining in on the fun. The girl sat on the empty hospital bed beside Francie's and stared out the window. Nixie hugged her brother and sister-in-law and sat down beside Stephanie.

After Boone shook Ryan's hand and complimented the new mother, he took a seat on the bed, sandwiching Stephanie between him and Nixie. Stephanie didn't seem happy about it.

For a while, talk centered around Merrilee's birth and Francie's health. Nixie smiled to see the pride that shone on her brother's face. She imagined Boone's reaction would be similar if he were in Ryan's shoes.

Then her thoughts led her into a detailed daydream in which she, rather than Francie, was the new mother. Her parents were due to arrive from Baltimore later this evening, and Nixie imagined them joining the rest of her loved ones in this room to rejoice in the child who was born as a result of her and Boone's love for each other. She wouldn't even care whether it was a girl or a boy, as long as the baby had Boone's good qualities.

"Chad was telling us things are looking pretty serious between you two," said Francie.

Nixie glanced up and caught the look that passed between Aunt Laura and Uncle Jim. Chad, Ryan and Francie smiled approvingly. Only Stephanie looked glum. Staring down at her hands, the girl refused to join in the conversation.

Boone reached behind Stephanie and covered Nixie's hand with his own. "Yes, but Nixie tells me that when a man marries a woman, he marries the family, as well."

Ryan laughed. "You're right. I never realized what I was up against when I married into Francie's family."

Francie gave her husband a playful punch.

Boone shrugged. "Well, I've asked her, but—"

"Boone! This isn't the time or place."

"But, honey, most of your family's right here. You may as well find out right now how they feel about us getting married."

"All for the lovebirds tying the knot," Uncle Jim piped up, "raise your hand."

This was not turning out at all as she had expected. Nixie had planned to have a private talk with Stephanie and Chad before announcing their intentions to the rest of the family.

Hands went up, including Boone's. Stephanie stared sullenly into her lap.

"All opposed?" Chad continued.

Everyone turned and waited for the lone holdout's response. Stephanie made an obvious show of concentrating on picking off the remains of her pink nail polish.

"Abstaining, huh?" Boone gave Stephanie's hair a little tug. "I'll bet you're just playing hard to get. Right, Steph?"

Nixie was startled speechless when her daughter stood in front of Boone, hands defiantly on her hips, and declared, "My name is Stephanie, not Steph." Turning to Chad, she added, "And I wish we'd never placed that stupid ad."

Then, wiping the moisture from her eyes, she ran out into the hall.

Nixie didn't know what to do first—apologize to Boone or run after her daughter. And if she went after Stephanie, should she comfort her or chew her out?

Although Boone started to follow her, Nixie stayed him with a hand on his arm. "Give me a minute alone with her." She had expected to see the hurt on his face, and it was there. But he seemed more concerned about Stephanie's unhappiness. "I'm sorry about the way she's been acting lately. She's not usually like this."

He didn't say anything. Just nodded his understanding.

Out in the hall, Nixie started to scold her daughter for being so rude. Stephanie had lifted the hem of her shirt to wipe the tears from her eyes. Nixie's attention was drawn to the bare abdomen covered with hideous red splotches. When Stephanie kept rubbing her eyes with the shirt, Nixie pulled the girl's hands away from her face and discovered a large red hive covering most of her right eyelid.

"How long have you been itching?"

Stephanie rubbed her eye with the back of her hand, exposing more hives on her wrist. "Since before we got to the hospital. I thought it would go away." She wriggled her shoulders as if her back itched, too. "Mom, why is this happening?"

Nixie had her suspicions, but if she was wrong, she didn't want to give her daughter any ideas. If, indeed, Stephanie was reacting to the stress associated with her unwillingness to accept Boone as her stepfather, Nixie wanted to get to the root of the child's fears rather than hand her an excuse for them.

She hugged her daughter. "I don't know," she said at last. "But we're going to find out why, and we're going to come up with a solution."

Boone took them home, where they repeated the treatment Nixie had used the night before. It was obvious he wanted to help and was frustrated by his inability to do so.

"Let me take her to the emergency room," he urged.

Nixie rescued Stormy from another swat by Precious and put the kitten in the utility room. "It's not a life-threatening situation," she told him. "If she has another episode tomorrow, I'll take her to the doctor."

In the end, he reluctantly accepted her decision. He also accepted her refusal to let him spend the night and help take care of Stephanie.

Nixie hated sending him away. It meant a lot having someone to share her concern. True, she had Uncle Jim and Aunt Laura who fussed over the children constantly. And her parents, who were staying at Ryan and Francie's house, would have gladly helped. But, somehow, it was different with Boone. It was as if their shared concern over the children somehow brought them closer together.

She shook her head at the irony of it. If she was right in her suspicion that Stephanie's hives came from her unwillingness to accept Boone into the family, her child's illness could have the effect of driving them apart.

By morning, the hives had once again miraculously disappeared. When the children got off the school bus that afternoon and stormed into the sign shop, Nixie let Chad play a game on one of the computers while she took Stephanie into her office.

Nixie sat beside her daughter on the office couch and studied her carefully. No sign of hives on the exposed skin of her face, arms or legs. "How have you felt today?"

"Fine."

"Are you itching now?"

"Nope."

Both times Stephanie had broken out in the rash, she'd been hearing talk about the possibility of Nixie and Boone getting married. Nixie didn't want to bring on another episode for her daughter, but she had to know what was causing it. And this would be one way to find out.

"You know Boone asked me to marry him," she began.

"So did you tell him yes? Majority rules, you always say."

No sign of scratching yet. So far, the only thing Stephanie was suffering from was a sarcastic mouth. Deciding to concentrate on only one problem at a time, she ignored the tone of her daughter's voice.

"Yes, in most cases the majority rules. Before I give Boone my answer, I want to make sure it's a decision we'll *all* be happy with."

Stephanie idly twirled a lock of hair around her forefinger. "Are you saying this time it has to be unanimous?"

"I'm saying I want Boone to be a part of our lives, and I want you and Chad both to accept him as your father." Nixie reached over and pulled Stephanie's hand away from her hair. "I love him very much, Stephanie, and I want you to be happy for me."

"But it's not right," she cried, withdrawing her hand. "He's not my father, and he can't take anyone else's place."

"No one will ever take the place of your real father," Nixie assured her. "Not for you or Chad, and not for me, either."

"Well, maybe we don't need anyone else in our family."

Nixie wished she could understand what was going on in her daughter's mind. She didn't want to push too hard and make her retreat into a sullen silence. Nixie's voice automatically lowered as when she dealt with frightened patients at rescue calls. "I thought you liked Boone."

"It's not that..." Stephanie scratched her cheek, then started twisting her hair again. "You said that if Precious couldn't learn to accept Stormy, then we should find another home for the kitten. Well, Precious knows there are enough pets in our house. I've been in the family a lot longer than Boone has been around, and I know there are enough people in our house. Why can't you give me the same respect that you give our cat?''

Stephanie was near tears, and Nixie tried for a little levity. "You want me to take Boone to the animal shelter?''

It didn't work. Further, Nixie noticed that the spot where Stephanie had scratched her cheek was now turning a bright shade of red.

"We're giving Precious and Stormy a chance to work out their differences. The least I can do is give you and Boone the same courtesy.'' She patted her daughter's knee. "Now promise me you'll give it a try. If things work out as well as I expect they will, you can even be my maid of honor. Isn't that exciting?''

Stephanie gave her a listless shrug.

"I knew you'd be open-minded about this,'' Nixie said, trying for positive reinforcement. But she had her doubts about whether it was working.

Nixie sat Stephanie down at the desk to begin her homework and left to tell Chad to get started on his. Then she picked up a job order for a sale flyer and started typesetting it on the computer.

She'd been at it for less than fifteen minutes when Stephanie appeared at her elbow.

"Mom, the itching's back, and it feels kind of hard to breathe.''

Her eyes were swollen, and she was scratching frantically under the waistband of her shorts.

"Oh, heavens.''

Calling out instructions to Uncle Jim, she left him in charge of the shop and asked him to see that Chad got his homework done while she took Stephanie to the doctor.

Outside, Nixie fumbled through the first-aid kit she kept in the car in a futile attempt to locate some antihistamine. It wasn't something she ordinarily stocked, but she looked again anyway. When she turned up empty-handed, she urged Stephanie in the passenger side and pushed the speed limit to the doctor's office.

She didn't want to panic Stephanie, but a severe case of hives left untreated could cause the throat to swell shut. She had wanted to know if Stephanie's hives came from her stress about Boone joining the family. She had her answer, but she wished she had never tried the test.

Not only did she have her answer about Stephanie's feelings regarding the marriage, she had managed to set off a bad reaction. Guilt stabbed at Nixie's conscience.

The nurse let Stephanie go ahead of the handful of patients sitting in the waiting room. A few minutes later, the doctor gave her an injection, and her breathing soon came easier.

"The swelling should go down within the next hour or two," Dr. Coffman told her.

Nixie motioned him into the hall. "What do you think could be causing these episodes?"

"Well, this is the allergy season, especially for people sensitive to grass pollen. But if she's never had seasonal sniffles before, that's probably not the cause. Perhaps she's allergic to some other substance she has come in contact with."

"Nothing's different other than me dating someone special." Nixie started thinking aloud. "For a while I had this crazy idea she might be allergic to *him,* but today he was nowhere around. Although you know, each time she developed these hives, there had been discussion about us getting married. Do you suppose there could be a connection?''

Their family doctor flipped back through Stephanie's chart. "I see that she had hives when she was three."

"Yes, that was after my husband died."

He made a note in the chart, then tucked the pen behind his ear. "Then I suppose it very well could be a case of nerves." Leaving the first pen above his ear, he reached for another from the counter and scribbled out a prescription. "I suggest you keep her calm, and make a note of what she's wearing, eating, touching, or talking about if it happens again." He handed her the prescription. "And if she has another bad reaction, you may need to inject her with this."

Nixie stared at the scrawled writing on the slip of paper. Just when she was learning to give Chad more freedom without panicking about his safety, Stephanie wound up having anxiety reactions.

Why couldn't things be simple?

Over the next couple of weeks, Stephanie had a few more reactions, but none were as severe as the first three episodes.

Nixie didn't share with Boone her suspicion about the cause of the rash because she was afraid he might step up his efforts to win Stephanie over. And Nixie was afraid the added pressure would only make the outbreaks worse.

As it was, she asked him to give her a while longer before expecting an answer to his proposal. Saying she wanted the children to grow used to the idea of her remarrying, she asked Boone to keep the subject low-key. True to his word, he said nothing else to them about becoming their new daddy.

But his promise didn't keep him from stealing kisses from Nixie when Stephanie and Chad weren't looking. And if he didn't have an excuse to stop by and visit, he called to chat, and the phone was usually passed to everyone in the family to say hello.

His good-night calls were the ones Nixie looked forward to most. By then, the children were in bed, and they were free to talk without interruption. In the evenings, it felt wonderful to unwind with the man she hoped someday to marry. They were such little things—sharing their day's events and laughing about things that wouldn't seem funny to people who weren't in love. And each night Boone whispered "I love you" in the darkness before hanging up.

Such little things, but they meant so much.

Unfortunately, it seemed as though the more firmly Boone rooted himself in their lives, the more frequently Stephanie's hives appeared. It was a good thing school was out for the summer because the daily doses of antihistamine tended to make the girl groggy.

"We can't keep going on this way," Nixie told her aunt and uncle when they came to visit one Saturday morning. "It's tearing me up to watch my little girl suffer from these skin rashes. Just when I think she's over it, she'll break out again after Boone calls or if she catches us kissing."

"She's been very clingy to Jim, too," said Aunt Laura.

Uncle Jim paused in his search through the kitchen junk drawer. "She followed me into the bathroom yesterday. I can't walk through a room without her hugging me and telling me she loves me." He grinned at her. "It's nice to know, but it does get tiresome after a while."

Nixie watched as her uncle withdrew a sheet of paper and began drawing a pair of large eyes on it. "On the other hand," she said, "Chad has been teasing her less and getting into less trouble with his pranks."

Uncle Jim snorted. "That's an improvement? My main man told me it's immature to play a lot of jokes on people."

"Imagine that," Aunt Laura said dryly. She winked at Nixie.

Jim finished the drawing and headed off toward the stairs.

"Where are you going with that?" she asked.

He stopped and grinned devilishly. "Gonna slide it under her bedroom door and make her feel like she's being watched."

Nixie shook her head. "How do you put up with him?" she asked Aunt Laura.

"You get used to checking whether the bed's been short-sheeted or the toilet seat is greased. It's a challenge to see if I can stay one step ahead of him."

She heard a squeal from upstairs and knew Uncle Jim had scored.

She and Aunt Laura had just settled down with a cup of coffee each when Boone joined them.

"The door was unlocked," he said in explanation as he helped himself to a cup of the steaming brew.

His inevitable shadow followed him into the kitchen. "What does a man have to do to get some coffee around here?" Chad asked with a mischievous grin. "Get drunk?"

Uncle Jim rejoined them, and he and Aunt Laura listened with amusement as Chad told them about the fermented fruit juice.

"What brings you here so early this morning?" Nixie asked after Chad had finished his tale.

"Friends of mine have opened a go-cart track over in Millbridge. I thought it would be fun if we drove over and watched some races." He turned to Laura and Jim. "Y'all come, too. The more, the merrier."

They declined, but Chad raced upstairs to tell Stephanie. He came back down after only a few minutes.

"Stephanie says she can't go because she's itching again."

Nixie sighed and stood up to get the medicine. As much as it broke her heart to acknowledge it, Stephanie very obviously was having nervous reactions to Boone's presence. How could she consider marrying Boone if her own daughter couldn't tolerate being in the same room with him?

With a heavy heart, she knew what she had to do.

She turned to Boone. "If you want to take Chad, that's okay with me. I'll stay home and look after Stephanie." Then, to Aunt Laura she said, "Would you mind watching the kids after Boone gets back? We need to talk."

As much as she hated to do it, she had no choice but to refuse his marriage proposal.

Chapter Nine

Boone just didn't understand it.

He and Chad had spent a great day at the go-cart track. The kid was good company, helping keep his mind off missing Nixie and Stephanie. Boone wished they'd been able to come, but he understood that being out in the heat would only make Stephanie's rash worse. Yet, he still missed them.

And it prickled at his conscience that he might be the cause of Stephanie's hives. She had been keeping him at arm's length lately, and it was obvious she didn't want him to marry her mother. The confusing part was that, for the most part, she actually seemed to like him. Boone had never had trouble winning over kids before, maybe because he acted like a big kid himself. So why was he striking out with Stephanie?

But the really weird part was when Nixie had blown his socks off with her announcement that they weren't "compatible," and suggested they stop seeing each other.

Humph, "suggested" was too mild a word. "Demanded" was closer to the mark.

He'd been such an idiot. All during the races, he'd fantasized about being a part of the happy family. He'd daydreamed about sharing the mundane, everyday experiences with the woman he loved and the two children who had found a special place in his heart. He had daydreamed about arguing over whose parents they would visit on the holidays. And he'd rejoiced in the thought of never having to spend another night alone. It would be such heaven, he knew, to finally claim Nixie as his own. He would claim her with his declaration of love and devotion as he slipped the wedding band onto her slim finger, and he would claim her with his body every night thereafter.

While he'd spent the day thinking she'd planned some private time with him to accept his proposal and finish what they'd started on the couch a while back, she had actually been planning to drop a bombshell on him.

In a way, he was glad he hadn't known what was coming. When he and Chad had bought hot dogs at the concession stand, the matronly attendant had beamed at them both and declared how much Chad looked like his "father." Boone didn't know who was more pleased—he or Chad.

It had been such fun to pretend that Chad was his kid. Yep, he was glad he hadn't known what Nixie was going to hit him with that evening.

Boone reshuffled the papers on his desk and sorted them into stacks. He didn't know why he'd come to work today. He couldn't keep his mind focused on his work.

The thing that puzzled him most was that it was plain to see Nixie loved him. She hadn't said the words, but he could see it in her eyes. He'd gone over their conversation in his mind a hundred times since then, and he was convinced it wasn't just wishful thinking on his part. It was plain to see that Nixie wanted him as much as he wanted her.

The only plausible explanation for her refusal of his marriage proposal was Stephanie. Why wouldn't Nixie open up and be honest with him? he wondered. Why didn't she realize he could help her overcome Stephanie's opposition to the marriage? He didn't blame Nixie for putting her family first. He probably would have done the same. But he just wished she hadn't handed him that malarkey about not being compatible—that they knew in high school they weren't right for each other and that they were trying to fool themselves now.

Boone ripped open the envelope on top of the stack of incoming mail.

He would be seeing her tonight at his office—a distancing ploy on her part, he was certain—to discuss the donkey-ball game she was planning as a fund-raiser for the rescue squad. And Boone was determined to use his powers of persuasion on her. He wasn't about to give up without a fight.

Despite her brave words to the contrary, Nixie loved Boone and missed him desperately. She could tell Chad missed his rambunctious friend, too. As for Stephanie, she'd turned even more moody and depressed.

Nixie was glad to see her rash disappear. After she'd told the children she wouldn't marry Boone, Stephanie had suffered no more hives outbreaks. Nixie had expected the news would cheer her daughter up, but the girl became even more withdrawn.

Nixie was stumped. Stephanie, who usually chattered a mile a minute, now spoke in monosyllables. The longest conversation Nixie had heard her daughter conduct these past few weeks had been with Precious, the cat.

They had all decided that since Precious and Stormy couldn't smooth out their differences, the kitten would have to go. Nixie had gone upstairs to put freshly laundered and folded clothes in Chad's room when she heard her daughter carrying on a conversation.

There were no visitors at the house that she might be talking to. Out of curiosity, Nixie laid the clothes on Chad's bed and shamelessly eavesdropped on her daughter in the next room.

"Don't you worry, Precious," Stephanie said in her most soothing voice, "we're going to send that bothersome Stormy to live with someone else.

"I wish you could have gotten along with him, because he really is a funny kitten." She was quiet a moment, and Nixie guessed she was laying her cheek against the animal's fur just as she'd always done when she needed comforting. "But I'm your favorite person, and you don't want to hurt my feelings by being friends with Stormy. Do you? Of course you don't."

There was another short silence before she continued her chat with the cat. "I know just how you feel. Uncle Jim is one of my favorite people—even if he does play tricks on me all the time."

Chad came bursting into the room. "Hey, Mom! Steven called, and he wants me to come to his house tonight. Will you drop me off before you go to that meeting about the donkey-ball game?"

Stephanie came into the room, still clutching Precious. "I want to stay with Aunt Laura and Uncle Jim."

"Sure," Nixie told them. "But you two have swimming lessons in the morning, so we won't stay late."

She said that more for her own benefit than for the children's. Meeting with Boone, as she would be doing tonight, she wanted to limit the amount of time she would spend with him.

She'd felt guilty, lying to him as she had. She knew they were as compatible as two people could be. But she couldn't let Stephanie be the fall guy for their breakup. If she'd told Boone the real reason—that Stephanie was against the marriage and that Nixie couldn't marry him if it meant choosing between her own happiness and her family's—he would have tried to win Stephanie over. And that would have only increased the nervous tension she was suffering from.

Maybe, in a way, she hadn't lied about their compatibility after all. In truth, if Boone wasn't compatible with the entire family, then he wasn't compatible with her.

Nixie just wished the truth didn't hurt so much.

They were going over the final details of their publicity plans for the donkey-ball game. Jeff, the rescue worker who had been with Nixie the day Boone had been hit by the car, had agreed to head the committee to find a site for the event and invite local business owners to play for a fee. Nixie and Boone were in charge of publicity, with Nixie making flyers to put in store windows and Boone designing and running public service advertisements as well as a feature article in his newspaper.

Nixie had trouble concentrating on the display ad spread on the table before them. Instead she was wondering why she had ever mailed that letter to the advice columnist, "Ask Aunt Alice."

The letter had started as a way for Nixie to organize her thoughts about what was going on between her and Boone. She had hoped that seeing the situation in black and white would help her find a solution to the dilemma she was in. After she had covered both sides of three sheets of notebook paper, she had impulsively addressed an envelope to the *Lakewood Gazette*'s answer lady and dropped the letter into the big blue mailbox in front of the grocery store.

She'd had second thoughts about sending a stranger such a personal letter the minute it slipped from her fingers and slid down the mail chute. At least she'd had the good sense not to sign her name. She just hoped the columnist wasn't familiar enough with the people of Lakewood to connect her name with the return address on the outside of the envelope.

Nixie looked up at Boone as he flipped through a clipart book in his search for an illustration of a donkey. It amazed her how such a slight motion could make the oversize muscles in his arm flex and bunch. She longed to lay her hand on his arm, feel the strength beneath her fingertips, and tell him she'd made a terrible mistake when she'd refused his marriage proposal.

But the look on his face was one of businesslike concentration. His whole attitude this evening had been aloof, and his body language clearly said "Keep your distance."

She didn't blame him. He'd been hurt. Why should he open himself up for more of the same?

"Jeff saved a position for you to play in the donkey-ball game," she said. In answer to the empty stare she received from Boone, she added, "It seemed only fair, what with all you've contributed to the planning and advance publicity. The sporting goods store is contributing T-shirts with the names of the businesses represented by each player. You'll need to call them soon to let them know your size."

He just nodded. The only hint of emotion on his face was the jerk of a muscle in his jaw.

Nixie had seen the gesture many times before, but she'd never been the cause of it until now. She had seen it the time a school bully had mocked the slurred words of a partially deaf student. He'd reacted this way when his favorite teacher had told the class she'd been diagnosed with cancer. And then there was the time he'd seen his sister dancing too close to Robert Gage, the ninth-grade heartthrob.

The muscle twitched again in Boone's jaw. "Do you want to use the picture that looks like a nativity scene donkey, or the comical one with the ears as long as his body?"

"Let's use the comical one," Nixie said, trying to ignore his brusque tone. "It should lure more people to come see the fun."

She wondered how much fun the game would be if he were still treating her like a business associate. But why should she expect anything different? She was the one who'd insisted she didn't want a personal relationship with him. He was merely giving her what she'd asked for.

There was another hour or so of stilted questions and answers before the rough-sketched ad looked as eye-catching as they could possibly make it.

Nixie stood, stretched, and reached for her purse when Boone intercepted her hand with his own.

His voice was so low Nixie had to strain to hear him. "You can't go on pretending."

She pulled her hand back, but he refused to let go. "I don't know what you mean."

"You know exactly what I mean." His eyes narrowed to angry slits that dared her to argue. "You're not a good liar, Nixie. You can't pretend you don't love me."

He was right. She'd never been a good liar, partly for lack of practice, but mostly because it didn't set well with her to deceive anyone. Maybe she could hedge her way around the admission he was trying to extract from her.

She felt as though she were slapping him when, finally, after an interminable silence, she said softly, "I never told you I love you."

He looked stunned, and his grip on her hand loosened. Unwilling to witness the damage she'd inflicted on his soul, Nixie started to turn away but was stopped with a brick-hard hand on her shoulder. When she still refused to look at him, he grasped her other shoulder and forced her to face him.

Then he kissed her with the passion of a man who saw only one chance to win back his lady's love. His determination was evident in the savage hunger of his questing lips. His hands slid from her shoulders and traveled down her sides, slowing at the slight curve of her breasts and coming to rest at the small of her back.

Nixie resisted at first, determined to deny her attraction to him. But the rightness of it, the feel of him plundering her lips—her very soul—was enough to weaken her. The muscles in the back of her knees seemed to turn to rubber, and she swayed against him. Though she hadn't thought it possible, he pulled her closer.

Under the aggressive play of his lips on her mouth, her hands relaxed from balled-up fists and slid upward around his neck.

He was far from gentle, and Nixie welcomed his roughness. His hand moved up and clutched the hair at the back of her head, preventing her retreat from the demanding possession of his ravenous kiss.

But he didn't need the force of his muscles to restrain her. She was already under his spell and had been for many years. His two-day beard rasped against her cheek, but Nixie didn't care. She wanted to envelop herself in his embrace and enjoy the warmth of his touch, the quick puffs of his breath on her skin, his overwhelming presence.

Her breathing was coming in shallow, ragged pants. She was keenly aware of his firmness pressing against her belly, eliciting a warmth that radiated from the center of her being. She arched back, exposing her neck to the wonders that his lips played upon her sensitive skin.

Just as suddenly as he had initiated the kiss, Boone released her with a shocking abruptness. Still giddy from the closeness they'd just shared, Nixie clung to him, but Boone coldly pushed her away.

Though his lips were still reddened from their pillaging forays, they were now pressed into a tight, thin line. Through the haze of her emotions, Nixie was confused at the unexpected change of attitude.

He was still breathing hard, his chest rising and falling in a rhythm that tempted her to work loose the buttons on his shirt. "Now," he said through harsh breaths, "if you can tell me honestly that you don't care for me, I'll never bother you again."

Against her will, Nixie looked up into the blue eyes that dared her to deny her feelings. If she admitted the truth, she'd be choosing her own personal happiness over the well-being of her family. She had always put her family first, no matter what. And she couldn't betray them now.

Her gaze dropped from his, and she told the biggest lie of her life.

"We're not suited for each other, Boone." Taking a deep breath, she continued. "The obstacles are too big for us. Let's just forget we ever considered a serious commitment."

She couldn't bring herself to say the word "marriage," but she knew Boone understood her meaning. She could tell by his crushed look of defeat.

Ashamed of what she'd done to such a wonderful man, she turned and fled from his office.

Over the next couple of weeks, Nixie saw Boone once when she dropped off an update sheet on the donkey-ball game and twice when he stopped by the house to pick up Chad for Scout meetings. The other dens weren't meeting during the summer, but Boone had reasoned the boys would welcome the chance to see their friends and get a head start on earning next year's badges.

To his credit, Boone acted toward the children as though nothing had happened between him and Nixie. She had tried to make herself scarce during his short visits, and during those times he had spent his time mumbling to Tarzan while he waited for Chad to find his Scout manual. Nixie wondered if Boone were just being friendly to the bird or if, like Stephanie, he found it easier to pour his heart out to one of God's creatures than to confide in another human.

When the day of the donkey-ball game finally arrived, Boone was there early, setting out bases on the baseball diamond behind the high school. As one of the business owners who would be playing in the game, Boone wasn't required to be there early. Even though Jeff had reserved a position for him in exchange for the free advertising in his newspaper, Boone had made a pledge to the rescue squad. When business owners around the county had asked for the opportunity to play in the game, Boone had suggested Nixie put the positions up for bids. For his contribution, Boone doubled that of the top bidder. The money would go to a good cause—switching over to the Enhanced 911 emergency dispatch system. It was a project close to Nixie's heart, and even in such an indirect way, Boone was glad for the chance to help make her happy.

Boone returned to the ticket booth where Nixie was instructing a volunteer on the prices to charge for children and adults. Ever since he'd arrived this evening, she had been frantically running from place to place, trying to make sure every detail was taken care of.

As she turned to rush off and flag down another volunteer, Boone caught her around the waist and pulled her to him. Ignoring her look of surprise, he lowered his voice so the ticket taker couldn't hear. His words laden with innuendo, he whispered, "Tell me what I can do for you."

Just like old times, Boone thought as she blushed prettily. But this time, instead of wishing and wondering if she cared for him, he knew for a fact that the blush came less from embarrassment than from her own repressed desire for him.

Yes, indeed, he had solid evidence that Nixie loved him. Boone planned to press his advantage and force her to admit it. Somehow he had to prove to her that the "obstacles" she'd cited were surmountable. He needed to prove that, between the two of them, they could leap all hurdles on their path to wedded bliss.

Just as he'd expected, she chose to take his words at face value. "You can see if the van with the donkeys has arrived yet."

"It pulled in a couple of minutes ago, and they're parking it in the outfield."

"Won't that be in the way?"

"Nah. The squishy ball they're using will keep the game near the infield."

As if suddenly aware of their proximity, she stepped back, away from the circle of his arms. Boone made no effort to stop her. She could keep physical distance from him, but he wouldn't let her push him away emotionally. "How are Stephanie and Chad?" he asked.

She lifted the damp bangs off her forehead, poked out her lower lip, and blew. "Fine. Uncle Jim and Aunt Laura will be bringing them soon. They've been looking forward to this for a long time."

"Precious and Stormy?"

She hesitated as if suspicious of his line of questioning. "We're going to have to find Stormy a new home. I've been putting it off, hoping he and Precious would learn to get along. But now the kids have become attached to him."

Boone shoved his hands into his jeans' pockets. "I'm sorry. If I'd known, I would have insisted on taking the kitten with me that day I found him under your bush."

"It's okay." Automatically, she touched his arm.

Yes, Boone thought, she really did care for him.

"Aunt Laura said she and Uncle Jim would take him if it didn't work out. And the kids would still get to play with him."

Boone nodded. "And Tarzan? Has he learned any new words lately?"

Nixie smiled. Boone could tell she thought he was teasing her again with all his questions about the inhabitants of her house. She rested her hands on her back pockets, and Boone enjoyed the way the movement made her shirt adhere to her breasts.

"He hasn't learned any new words," she said, "but Stephanie's been threatening to teach him to say 'Here kitty kitty.'"

Boone chuckled at the thought. "It would serve the bird right for all those times he made the cat jump when he barked at her." He looked at her, probing her eyes with his gaze. "And how about Nixie? Is she happy?"

Boone didn't miss how her smile faltered momentarily.

"I'm keeping busy." She looked around them at the people who were starting to arrive. "It looks like we'll have packed bleachers for the game. And I'm happy that we'll be making lots of money for the new emergency dispatch system."

She hadn't said she was happy at home. Or at night when she crawled between the sheets of that big, lonely double bed. Boone was glad she wasn't trying to deceive herself into believing she was happy without him.

That was half the battle won. To win the other half, Boone would have to get her to openly admit that she still loved him. And if he could win the battle, he'd have a better chance at claiming the ultimate victory... getting her to say yes to marrying him.

Later, as Nixie tugged at the halter of her recalcitrant donkey, she tried not to think about the man watching her from astride his mount at first base. Although the bleachers were packed with laughing fans, many of them calling advice to her, Nixie was unmindful of them. That one man had the power to make her feel self-conscious when all the others combined did not.

Each donkey had been trained to have a different personality. The animal's name she had drawn out of the hat had been Flash, so it had come as a surprise to discover that the little beast didn't live up to her name.

If she couldn't get the donkey to its place beyond the batter's box within the allotted amount of time, Nixie would lose her turn at bat, earning an automatic out.

And the rescue squad and fire department couldn't afford that. The business owners had pledged to pay for every point the emergency crew scored over the opposing team. Nixie let go of the halter and walked around to the back of the animal. Giving a push, she was grateful for the donkey's mild-mannered disposition.

Gradually, with agonizing slowness, Nixie urged Flash to her appointed box. When the donkey's hoof touched the chalk line, a cheer rose up from the bleachers. Taking the rubber bat in hand, Nixie stepped up to the batter's box.

She glanced at the first baseman and squelched a giggle. The biggest man on the Lakewood merchants team, Boone had drawn the name of Tiny, the smallest donkey. In an effort to reduce the weight on the animal, Boone balanced on one leg with the other draped over Tiny's back.

Winding up, the pitcher tossed the ball. Nixie made two strikes before she finally hit the padded ball with a dull thud. It rolled no more than twenty feet.

Players flew to action as they all raced for their mounts. Nixie clambered onto Flash's back and urged her toward first base. The donkey plodded along as though she were on a Sunday stroll.

Up ahead, Nixie could see the pitcher had thrown toward Boone, who missed it when Tiny came to an abrupt stop just shy of the ball. With difficulty, Boone turned his donkey and—half riding, half hopping—raced toward the ball. Just as Boone was leaning to pick it up, Tiny knocked it with her front hoof, kicking it out of reach.

Meanwhile, Flash plodded steadily toward first base.

By now, the second baseman had figured out that his mount went left when urged right and right when steered left. By leaning in the opposite direction of where he wanted to go, he managed to work his way toward first base to back up Boone.

Nixie bounced up and down on Flash's back, nudged her sides with the heels of her sneakers, and gently swatted her rump. No matter what she did, the animal never changed course or speeded up. But it didn't matter because the other riders were just as disadvantaged as she.

Just as Flash was moseying up to the plate, Boone attempted to grab the ball and turn his miniature steed toward her. Hopping and flailing his arms, he managed to keep up with the swift-footed animal beneath him.

As they doggedly raced toward her, Nixie feared less that she'd score an out than that she'd get run over. When they were a few feet from her, Nixie cringed and waited for the inevitable impact.

It never came. Bracing her little hooves in the dirt just beyond reach of the plate, Tiny came to another bone-jarring halt. In his enthusiasm to tag Nixie out, Boone had apparently forgotten his mount's annoying personality trait. He pitched forward from the momentum, doing a half flip before landing flat on his back.

In a hurry to leave the damage she'd caused, Tiny jumped over her rider and headed toward the outfield to grab a mouthful of clover.

"Boone!" Nixie had heard his audible "Oomph!" when he hit the ground. Forgetting about making sure Flash's hoof touched first base, forgetting about the importance of scoring points to help earn more money for the squad, forgetting everything but the thought that Boone might be hurt as he lay motionless on the ground, Nixie jumped down and ran to him.

"Boone! Boone, are you all right?" Kneeling beside him, she resisted the urge to lift his head and cradle him in her arms. From her experience running calls with the squad, she knew he could have sustained a serious injury. He may have damaged a vertebra the way he'd fallen so hard. Or he could have broken his neck or suffered a concussion.

Grabbing his wrist, she checked for a pulse. "Come on, Boone, you can't do this to me," she whispered. "Please tell me you can hear me." When he remained deathly still, Nixie felt a tear slide down her cheek. "Oh, God, Boone, I couldn't stand it if anything bad happened to you."

The other players had abandoned their donkeys, as well, and now circled them. "Is he breathing?" someone asked.

His eyes were shut, and in her panic Nixie couldn't detect whether his chest was rising and falling as it should. She laid a hand on the hard planes of his chest and leaned closer to see if she could feel his breath against her cheek.

Someone shushed the crowd, but even so, she couldn't detect any sign of respiration. She glanced at his handsome face and decided to listen again before beginning life-saving techniques. She put her ear close to his mouth.

His breath came out in a short, quick puff against her face. Startled at the unexpected response, she jerked around and looked into his smiling eyes.

"Go ahead and admit it, Nixie. You *do* love me."

Chapter Ten

He had set her up. And Nixie had fallen for it like a row of dominoes.

It was Saturday morning, the day after Boone's hoax, yet she still couldn't stop thinking about the scare he'd given her. And the awkward part was that, with all those people crowded around them, she couldn't deny what he had said. All she could do was drown him with her tears of relief and promise him that if he ever pulled another stunt like that she'd personally give him a concussion.

Jeff finished backing the ambulance into the squad building's bay. Nixie got out and pressed the button to lower the automatic door. Thanks to it being a weekend, they'd managed to pick up a third volunteer, Marvin, who had helped considerably on the rescue call.

"I'm glad old Mr. Binford is going to be all right," Marvin said. "The way he was breathing, he had me pretty worried."

Nixie chuckled as she recalled their trip to the emergency room with the elderly man gasping for breath. It wasn't until Marvin had started questioning the man's daughter that they discovered the reason for his breathing problem. At age eighty-nine, Mr. Binford was unable to get around as much as he used to, so his daughter had installed cable television for him to watch. The old man had clicked through the channels until he found a program featuring women wrestlers. After a few moments of viewing, he had hyperventilated.

"I wish all our calls were this easy. Fix the problem, then cart 'em to the hospital to be checked out." Nixie snapped her fingers. "Just like that."

A few minutes later, as she pulled into her driveway, Nixie decided she'd have to tell Uncle Jim what happened to Bo Binford. She checked the mailbox and found one envelope. The return address was that of the *Lakewood Gazette*. Something from Boone?

With tentative fingers, she opened the letter. It was from Aunt Alice, the advice columnist. Nixie had almost forgotten she'd sent that letter in which she'd poured out her frustrations. Too late, she realized the embarrassment she could have caused if the letter had been used in the newspaper column. Thank goodness Aunt Alice had chosen to reply personally.

Dear Reader,

It appears your daughter did, indeed, want a father, but perhaps she expected a generic man who could be a companion to her mother and a helper to her and her brother. From what you told me in your letter, it seems she didn't expect to involve her heart any more than if she were hiring a gardener. Yet, things turned out differently than she expected, and she began to love this man who recently re-entered your life. Have you considered that she may feel disloyal to her deceased father by loving another man?

Nixie stared at the letter in amazement. She had been trying for weeks to figure out what was bothering Stephanie, and the only thing she could conclude was that her daughter was just as confused by her reaction to Boone as she was. And yet an advice columnist—a complete stranger—was able to sum up the problem in a mere paragraph. Nixie couldn't help being astonished by the writer's perception and insight.

The letter concluded with:

Remember that children don't always know what's best for them. Be honest with the man you love and tell him what you told me. With the help of his love and understanding, both of you can help your daughter cope with her ambiguous feelings.

For the next several days Nixie's thoughts kept returning to Alice's letter. Why hadn't she seen that Stephanie's resistance reflected her loyalty to her father's memory? Nixie supposed she had overlooked that possibility because Stephanie had been so young when Paul died.

One thing was certain. Stephanie had been receptive to Boone and enjoyed his friendship until they'd begun talking about marriage. If her daughter had truly disliked him, Nixie's decision to break things off with Boone would have been a little easier to bear. But she knew that Stephanie cared for him as much as Chad did. That was what made things so frustrating.

Her heart ached as she thought of the pain she'd put Boone through. But, she reminded herself, she hadn't known what else to do at the time.

Nixie walked into the living room and noticed that Chad had forgotten to cover Tarzan before he went to bed. Pulling the cloth up over the bird's cage, she whispered, "Night-night."

"Night-night," the parrot echoed. Then the bird whispered a phrase she'd never heard him say before. In fact, she'd never heard the loudmouth whisper until now.

She listened closely, waiting for him to repeat the phrase. When he did, she couldn't believe her ears.

"Boone loves Nixie," the bird confided in a hushed croak.

Shocked, Nixie echoed the statement as if to verify what she'd just heard. "Boone loves Nixie?"

Tarzan sidestepped closer on his perch and peered at her through the bars with one beady eye. "Boone loves Nixie," he whispered several times in succession. Then he shocked her back to reality by shrieking, *"Ha-ha-ha-ha-ha-ha-ha-ha."* Stunned, Nixie finished covering the cage.

"Night-night," Tarzan peeped. Then he began quietly practicing the new sentence he'd just mastered.

Her mind still reeling, she stumbled into the kitchen to catch Stormy and lock him up for the night. Warm with emotion from the bird's whispered revelation, Nixie hugged the little brown kitten. "Boone loves Nixie," she said to the squirming animal. "That must have been what he was mumbling to Tarzan all those times I found him by the cage."

The advice columnist's suggestion came back to her. *Be honest with the man you love.* Although she loved Boone with all her heart, she'd never told him—not even after his tumble at the donkey-ball game. He would be coming tomorrow to take Chad to the den meeting. She'd tell him then. She'd also enlist his aid in helping Stephanie cope with her "ambiguous feelings."

For the first time in a long while, Nixie's spirits soared. There was hope, after all. And that hope empowered her, made her sense that, together, she and Boone could accomplish anything—they could even make Stephanie realize there was room in their family, and in her heart, for a newcomer such as Boone.

Precious rubbed against her legs, demanding a bedtime snack. Putting Stormy down on the floor, Nixie reached into the pantry and retrieved a can of the cat's favorite flavor, chicken chunks in sauce. She opened the can and turned to get their bowls. Precious stood in front of Stormy with her back arched and fur standing on end. The yellow cat bared her teeth and hissed at the newcomer.

"Stop that," Nixie said, stamping her foot at Precious. Remembering the overheard conversation Stephanie had with her cat, she wished there was a way to get the animals to become friends. Maybe if her daughter saw that Precious could accept an animal newcomer, then Stephanie could accept a human one.

As she started scooping the smelly stuff into the cat's dish, an idea occurred to Nixie. It was a farfetched idea, but at this point Nixie was willing to try anything.

Ignoring the angry hisses from Precious, she picked up the lanky kitten and cuddled him close. "Please excuse what I'm about to do to you," she told the brown feline. "If this works, we'll both be thanking each other."

That said, Nixie plunged her fingertips into the gravy-like sauce. Cooing all the while to the bewildered kitten, she stroked its head and left a patch of sauce smeared on its fur. "On the other hand, if this doesn't work," she told him, "I'll have to give you the added indignity of a bath."

A few more strokes, and Stormy was covered with cat food sauce from his eyebrows to his ear tips and down his neck. "Please let this work," Nixie murmured as she set him on the floor near Precious.

The older cat hissed again. Precious suddenly stopped and leaned forward, sniffing suspiciously. Moving closer, she sniffed her tiny counterpart.

Anxious, Nixie stood ready to intervene if the old-timer should attack the kitten.

Slowly, tentatively, Precious stretched until her mouth was at Stormy's neck. Nixie prayed fervently that Precious wouldn't do to the kitten what she had done to the chipmunk she'd caught last month.

When the yellow cat's tongue darted out to sample the aromatic kitten, Nixie breathed a sigh of relief. Soon Precious was happily cleaning the sauce off Stormy's head, and Stormy was obviously enjoying the older cat's rough massage. After the sauce was gone, instinct took over and Precious gave Stormy a thorough washing.

Nixie put her hands together, looked heavenward, and whispered a heartfelt "Thank you."

Later, after she'd dressed for bed, she went looking for Stormy, hoping she wouldn't have to lock him in the utility room again. After a thorough inspection of the house, she finally found him in Stephanie's room, snuggled on the ragged blanket that served as a bed for Precious. The older cat's yellow paw lay draped across the tiny kitten as they slept.

Nixie closed the door and went back to her bedroom. If only it could be this simple for Boone to win Stephanie's acceptance.

* * *

Wednesday evening, when Boone stopped by to pick up Chad for the Scout meeting, Nixie was ready for him.

Instead of pulling her hair back with clips as she often did to keep it out of the way, she'd spent a long time at the bathroom mirror, puffing her bangs and coaxing the reddish-brown locks into gentle waves that caressed her shoulders.

Even at her age, when she was old enough to know it didn't matter about the size of her endowments, she wished she had a little more on top. But she did have good legs, so she pulled on a pair of black stretch pants that would show them to their best advantage and topped it off with an oversize red shirt that fell below her hips.

Nixie had a lot to make up to Boone, and she wanted to give him every reason possible to forgive her for her foolish mistake. She only hoped it wasn't too late.

He prowled the den, waiting once again for Chad to gather his belongings together so they could go. Nixie was pleased that even though Boone seemed restless, he wasn't too distracted to notice the fit of her clothes. He gave her a once-over that would have earned any other man a slap for his familiarity. Coming from Boone, though, the intense observation made her feel twenty years old again—young, vibrant and alluring.

Nixie mentally reviewed her game plan, just as Boone had always done before going out on the football field. Remembering Aunt Alice's suggestion to be honest with the man she loved, she would begin by telling him her feelings for him. She'd follow by saying that, if he was still willing, she would welcome his presence—and especially his love and understanding—through the good times and bad in her life. And she'd be there for him through the good and bad times in his life.

She would have to warn him, though, that they needed to take things slowly with Stephanie. But, in doing so, that would give them time to learn more about each other and solidify their relationship before taking that giant step into marriage.

Boone's nervous prowling took him past Tarzan's cage. He paused and grinned at the bird. "Has he learned anything new recently?" he asked Nixie.

This was the opening she'd been waiting for. But first, she'd dish out a little of the teasing he'd given her so much of over the years. "Besides burping and excusing himself?"

Chad burst into the room with the subtlety of a train wreck. "I'm ready, Boone, let's go."

Boone caught the boy by the scruff of his shirt. "Wait a minute. What's your hurry?"

"He wants to get there first," Stephanie said, descending the stairs with ladylike poise, "because he wants to sit next to you."

"I can't blame him for that," Nixie said. An eyebrow raised, Boone turned and cast her a curious glance. Nixie met his gaze with a slight fluttering of her eyelashes. She hoped she wasn't overdoing it. Although he seemed encouraged by her response, she couldn't open the door to the discussion she'd planned—not with the children in the room.

"I have a surprise for all of you," Boone announced, reaching into his back pocket.

Chad crowded closer to his idol while Stephanie pretended little interest in the papers in his hand.

"Three more applicants," Boone said, holding the papers aloft.

Chad followed him to the sofa and sat down beside him, a frown creasing his youthful features. "I don't want a stranger for a daddy. I want *you.*"

Boone squeezed the boy's shoulder. Together, Nixie and Boone turned to Stephanie for her reaction.

The girl sat down beside her brother. Her expression was troubled, and Nixie couldn't help worrying that her daughter's discomfort might erupt in a physical form as it had done before.

"I'd like to see the letters," Stephanie told Boone.

Nixie's heart sank. When the pre-teen had awakened this morning to find Stormy and Precious playing together like the best of buddies, she had been ecstatic.

When Nixie had entered the room to find Stephanie playing with both cats, she had tried to point out to her daughter that Precious could accept Stormy and still love her. Nixie tried to make her realize, without coming right out and saying so, that Stephanie could accept Boone into her life and still love Paul.

Apparently the message hadn't sunk in.

Boone handed Stephanie the three letters. "I didn't think you'd get any more responses since the ad stopped running a long time ago," he told her. "These folks may have found an old newspaper lying around, or they might have planned to answer the ad but took a long time getting around to it."

Stephanie scanned the first letter while the three of them watched. After a moment she crumpled it into a ball, as she'd done with so many of the others. "This loser thinks it's okay to use drugs for 'recreational purposes,'" she said with a sneer in her voice.

Despite her disappointment that Stephanie was still unwilling to give Boone a chance, Nixie smiled her relief. Apparently the Just Say No message was firmly embedded in her daughter's attitude.

"How about the next one?" Boone asked.

Nixie blinked and glared at him with sharp disapproval. Why was he encouraging her? With a heavy sigh, she realized she couldn't blame him. After all, she'd been the one to tell him in no uncertain terms that there was no chance of a permanent relationship between them.

Stephanie opened the second letter in the stack. "This one's a farmer."

Apparently forgetting his earlier declaration about wanting only Boone for a daddy, Chad perked up and peered over his sister's shoulder. "Hey, maybe we could learn how to milk a cow!"

"Not this one," Stephanie said, tearing it in two. "He just wants us for extra help on the farm. *I'm* not going to ballet lessons smelling like cow dookie."

"Too late," Chad razzed, "you already do."

Nixie sought to soften the disappointment that was evident in her daughter's face. "Stephanie, this is why I was against your placing the ad for a daddy. It's hard enough to find a decent single man, and an ad such as yours and Chad's seems to bring responses from the people who are most desperate."

Stephanie scowled. "But I've seen articles in the newspaper about how people met through the want ads."

Nixie felt her daughter's pain. Sitting beside her, she put an arm around the child. "Those stories make the news because successes are so rare."

"Well, don't give up yet," Boone urged. "There's one more in your hand."

Nixie tried not to feel the pain that his words caused. He seemed too willing to find a replacement.

Stephanie's pessimism was obvious as she slowly opened the last letter, but her eyes widened as she pulled the letter from its envelope. "This one's typed."

"It's a long one, too," Chad piped in. "Read it out loud."

Stephanie cleared her throat and began.

Dear Children,

I am impressed by your enterprise, as well as your obvious high opinion of your mother. I trust she realizes how lucky she is to have thoughtful children such as yourselves.

Stephanie stopped and scratched her nose. "So far, so good. He must have good taste to recognize how wonderful we are." She smiled and continued.

Since beauty is in the eye of the beholder, I won't bother to describe my physical attributes. Why don't we let your mother decide for herself whether I meet her standards?

As for the other points you specified in your ad, I confess I strive to be strong in character as well as in physical fitness. I was raised in a loving home, and I look forward to sharing my love with a woman who wants to be my equal, yet is willing to accept that the differences in men and women serve to complement the whole.

Though I don't currently share my home with any animals, I am fond of all of God's creatures, especially children.

"God's creatures," Chad said. "He sounds like a

churchgoer.'' He licked his finger and stroked the air. ''That's another point for him.''

> You asked for someone who is dependable. I trust that you'll accept my ownership of a prominent business in your community as evidence that I am up to handling my responsibilities. Because of my professional endeavors, I must ask your understanding about my choosing to remain anonymous until your mother decides she'd like to meet me.

The letter ended with a suggestion they meet at seven o'clock Saturday night at an elegant restaurant just outside of town. Nixie would be able to identify the mystery man by the red carnation on his lapel.

''That's an expensive restaurant,'' Stephanie observed. ''I wonder if he's rich.''

''He used a bunch of big words,'' said Chad. ''I'll bet he's plenty smart enough for Mom.''

Boone leaned forward and looked past the children to catch Nixie's eye. ''This one sounds like a winner. Why don't you meet him?''

''Yeah,'' said Stephanie. ''It couldn't hurt.''

Chad got up and jerked his Scout manual off the lamp table. ''It sounds like a stupid idea to me.'' Turning to Boone, he added, ''Let's go, or we're going to be late.''

Boone rose slowly, passing Nixie a wink as he did so. ''Where's your sense of adventure, boy? I think it would be a good idea for your mother to meet this Mr. Wonderful.''

Nixie rose and followed them to the door. ''Boone, I don't think that's a good idea.''

"Hey, it's a great idea. If you're scared of meeting a stranger, I'll go and sit at another table to keep an eye on things."

"That won't be necessary, because I'm not going."

"What do you mean, you're not going? This guy has winner written all over him."

Nixie took a deep breath. Maybe she should go ahead and tell him now, in front of the children. Let him know she wasn't a lost cause where he was concerned. Silently she willed him to understand what she was trying so hard to communicate to him. "There's something important I have to tell you."

"We're going to be late. Let's talk when we get back. Meanwhile, mark your calendar for Saturday night. I want you to give this guy a try."

Nixie's throat closed at the cavalier manner in which he urged her to see another man. All she could manage to force out was one word. "Why?"

Boone stepped out onto the porch. Holding the screen door open, he gave a little shrug. "I want you and the kids to be happy."

Stepping into the shimmery black dress, Nixie turned around for Aunt Laura to zip it up.

"I ought to have my head examined," she told her aunt, "for agreeing to go out with a complete stranger."

Aunt Laura connected the hook and eye at the top of the dress and patted Nixie's back. "The mystery man sounds like quite a catch. Don't you think he's intriguing?"

Nixie nodded. He did, indeed, sound intriguing. Under other circumstances, she would have been more enthusiastic about meeting the man who'd sent that endearing letter. But her heart already belonged to Boone, and any other man paled in comparison.

She had been prepared to open her heart to Boone and let him know how much she cared for him. But by the time he'd brought Chad home from the Scout meeting, he had convinced her son that it was in her best interest to meet the man. Neither gave her an opportunity to say what was on her mind—and in her heart. And soon Stephanie was urging her to meet "Mr. Wonderful."

Nixie had cried herself to sleep that night. It hurt to know that the man she loved was trying so hard to get rid of her. He had obviously changed his mind about wanting to marry her, and though she considered begging him for another chance, she couldn't bring herself to do it.

She shaded her eyes as Aunt Laura tucked a stray bit of hair into the elaborate braid and sprayed it into place. "I won't be out late," Nixie said. "Please don't let Uncle Jim give the children too much junk food while I'm gone."

"Don't you worry about us. You just go and have a good time."

A good time. She doubted it. Nixie hoped Mr. Wonderful would be able to forgive her for ruining *his* evening. She was certain she wouldn't be very good company tonight. How could she, when she would spend the whole evening thinking about Boone?

"Park in a lighted area," Uncle Jim told her as she was leaving the house. "And ask the maître d' for a table that's out in the open where you can be seen by the other diners. Just in case he gets fresh, you know."

With a grin, Nixie pointed to her narrow-toed black shoes. "Don't worry. These should be a good deterrent."

She arrived too early at the restaurant. First, she'd overestimated how long it would take to get there. Then, in their eagerness, her family had whisked her out the door at least fifteen minutes sooner than she'd planned to leave.

Remembering her uncle's advice, she requested a table near the center of the restaurant. The waiter brought her a glass of white wine. She sipped it, hoping Mr. Wonderful would arrive soon so they could hurry and get this over with.

She was studying the wallpaper pattern when a flurry of activity caught her attention as a small group descended upon a nearby table. The boy caught her attention first. His blond hair was slicked back, and the kid sported a clip-on tie, white shirt and jeans.

Chad turned in his seat, grinned at Nixie and waggled his fingers in a friendly wave.

Chad! What was he doing here? And Stephanie... and Uncle Jim and Aunt Laura! The whole family had turned out to gawk at her mysterious stranger.

Nixie got up and walked over to their table. "Get a sudden craving for escargot?" she asked. "Or did you run out of videos and need something else to watch?"

Everyone started talking at once, making excuses for their unexpected appearance. It was obvious they had planned to come all along. How else could they have changed their clothes and arrived at the restaurant so soon after she did? Nixie gave them a beleaguered look.

Stephanie spoke up. "We'll be as quiet as mice. Just pretend you don't know us."

Uncle Jim and Aunt Laura murmured their agreement. Nixie met Aunt Laura's eyes. "It doesn't surprise me that Uncle Jim would show up here... but *you?*"

Aunt Laura gave her a guilty smile. "I couldn't help it, dear. I was just dying of curiosity."

After Aunt Laura assured her there would be no audible comments from the table and that they'd try not to stare, Nixie went back to her seat.

Taking another sip of the wine, she checked her watch. Six fifty-five. Her pulse was racing. Why was she so nervous about someone she didn't even want to meet? Nixie supposed it had something to do with the dread that settled over her. She felt guilty for wasting the man's time, not to mention his money, when she wasn't a bit interested in him. Checking her purse for a credit card, she decided the least she could do was pay for her own meal.

Someone appeared beside her with an armful of flowers. Nervous, Nixie stood and almost knocked over her chair. "Glad to meet—" In a split second she took in the dark, well-cut suit before her gaze traveled up to his face. "Boone! You, too?"

She took the flowers he offered her. Although she was touched by his show of support, she was beginning to feel like a circus sideshow.

"The flowers are a nice touch," she said. Glancing around the restaurant, she noticed a man who had just come in. Maybe that was Mr. Wonderful. The last thing she wanted to do was embarrass him with Boone's presence. "Look, maybe you should go now."

He grinned, but made no move to leave. Then Nixie noticed it.

The bright splash of red on his lapel.

As realization dawned on her, Nixie returned his grin. Boone was the mystery man.

Mr. Wonderful. His qualifications were perfect. Her aunt and uncle said so. Chad said so. Even Stephanie agreed that this latest candidate sounded like the perfect match for Nixie.

Nixie was pleased with this turn of events and knew it would thrill the rest of her family, but what about Stephanie?

Taking the bouquet from Nixie, Boone laid it on the table, then assisted with her chair as she took her seat. Nixie couldn't help experiencing a sudden giddiness that she knew was unrelated to the few sips of wine she'd had before he arrived.

Boone sat across from her and reached for her hand.

Nixie clasped his big fingers. "There's something I wanted to tell you last Wednesday."

"There will be plenty of time for that," Boone interrupted. "But, first, I have a couple of confessions to make."

Nixie's heart sank. Was he getting ready to play another joke on her?

"As you've probably already guessed, I'm the guy who wrote that last letter." With his free hand, he loosened the knot in his tie. "The other letters, though, were sort of . . . invented."

Nixie's thoughts tumbled through her brain. "You wrote them?" At his affirmative nod, she exploded. "Why would you do something like that? How dare you toy with my children's emotions!"

She tried to withdraw her hand from his grasp, but he held tight.

"Please. I wasn't trying to hurt your kids. I love them too much to do that." He took a sip of water, and it seemed as though he had a hard time swallowing. "I didn't want them to be disappointed when they didn't get any responses to their ad. Besides, it seemed like a good excuse for me to come and see you and the kids."

"So they were all fake."

Boone gave her a sheepish grin. "All but the one from the felon."

The waiter arrived, delaying their conversation for a moment. Nixie was glad for the interruption as it gave her time to collect her emotions.

Although she thought it was unwise for him to string them along as he had, she was convinced his intentions were pure. And, truthfully, she was glad things worked out the way they had.

As the waiter left with their orders, Boone made another startling revelation. "I'm Aunt Alice."

Nixie felt the blood drain from her face. "Oh, my gosh."

"I wish you had told me why you turned me down."

"If you knew, why didn't you say something?"

Boone looked down at his tie clip and fiddled with it before answering. "I figured you needed some space." Looking up, he added, "I still want you to marry me."

He was giving her another chance. She wasn't going to let it slip through her fingers again. "A very wise person once told me I should be honest with the man I love . . . and I do love you, Boone."

"Will you marry me?"

She answered without hesitation. "Yes."

"What about Stephanie? If she's still having a problem with us getting married, I don't want to cause another outbreak of hives."

Nixie had forgotten all about Stephanie's objections. Remembering Aunt Alice's sage advice, she acknowledged that children don't always know what's best for them. Somehow she'd have to convince her daughter that Boone would be a wonderful addition to the family.

"My answer will still be yes," she said, "but I want it to be with my family's blessing."

Excusing herself, Nixie went to the table where her family was eagerly observing their interchange. Uncle Jim pulled up a chair for her.

"Boone has asked me to marry him, and I want to tell him yes," she told her loved ones. Chad cheered, and Aunt Laura and Uncle Jim smiled at each other. "But not if it means causing divisiveness between me and my children."

Stephanie ducked her head and grabbed for a napkin to wipe her eyes.

"I think Stephanie and I need to go to the powder room," she told her family. "We'll be right back."

In the privacy of the rest-room lounge, Nixie spoke firmly with her daughter. Praying that Stephanie wouldn't have another outbreak of nerves, she told her how much she loved Boone. "Even you agreed he was the perfect candidate to be your dad. Don't you like Boone?"

Stephanie sobbed again, and Nixie handed her a fresh tissue.

"I do like Boone, and I want him in the family, but—"

"But what?"

"I don't want to hurt Uncle Jim's feelings."

Because she and her daughter were close, Nixie thought she'd understood Stephanie's reluctance to accept Boone. But her announcement shattered Nixie's assumption that Stephanie was merely being loyal to her father. *"Uncle Jim?"*

Stephanie nodded. "He always calls me his favorite little girl."

Nixie groaned. All along, Stephanie had been afraid of being disloyal to her uncle. She sat beside her daughter on the plush burgundy carousel. Maybe she could still make the cat analogy work. "Did you stop loving Precious when Stormy came along?"

"Of course not."

"Do you love Stormy more than you love Precious?"

"No. They're so different that it's hard to compare. I love Stormy because he's playful and funny, but I love Precious because she's sweet and she makes me feel better when I'm sad."

"Is Precious jealous when you play with Stormy?"

Stephanie threw her a suspicious look. "Not since they became friends." Suddenly she became enthusiastic. "You know, it's even more fun playing with both cats than just one at a time."

Nixie smiled. At last there was hope.

"Hey," said Stephanie. "Do you think it would be the same with Uncle Jim and Boone?"

Breakthrough! She tried to control her exhilaration as she and Stephanie walked back to the table. "Uncle Jim was willing to share you with Chad when he came along. I'm sure he wouldn't mind sharing you with Boone."

Stephanie gave her an impulsive hug.

As Nixie started back to Boone, she gave him a thumbs-up sign. She thought he was going to help her with her chair again, but instead he guided her back to her family's table and urged her to join them.

He dropped to one knee. His eyes were on Nixie, but his words addressed them all. "Will y'all marry me?"

The answer was a chorus of five yeses.

The tears that flowed from Nixie's eyes were tears of happiness. It had taken them fifteen years to realize they had loved each other all along. And now the people who were dearest to her agreed they belonged together. Nixie didn't think she'd ever been happier in her entire life.

Boone stood and urged her into his arms, the best place in the world for her to be.

Standing there, tears leaking onto his shirt, Nixie was aware that all eyes in the restaurant were upon them. But she didn't care. All that mattered was that she and Boone and her family were going to be together at last.

"It's unanimous," she whispered. "We'll marry you."

*   *   *   *   *

**HE'S MORE THAN
A MAN, HE'S
ONE OF OUR**

DADDY'S ANGEL
Annette Broadrick

With a ranch and a houseful of kids to care for, single father Bret Bishop had enough on his mind. He didn't have time to ponder the miracle that brought lovely Noelle St. Nichols into his family's life. And Noelle certainly didn't have time to fall in love with Brett. She'd been granted two weeks on earth to help Brett remember the magic of the season. It should have been easy for an angel like Noelle. But the handsome rancher made Noelle feel all too much like a woman....

Share the holidays with Bret and his family in Annette Broadrick's *Daddy's Angel,* available in December.

Fall in love with our **Fabulous Fathers!**

ROMANCE™

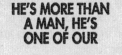

Take 4 bestselling love stories FREE

Plus get a FREE surprise gift!

Special Limited-time Offer

Mail to Silhouette Reader Service™

3010 Walden Avenue
P.O. Box 1867
Buffalo, N.Y. 14269-1867

YES! Please send me 4 free Silhouette Romance™ novels and my free surprise gift. Then send me 6 brand-new novels every month, which I will receive months before they appear in bookstores. Bill me at the low price of $1.99* each plus 25¢ delivery and applicable sales tax, if any.* That's the complete price and—compared to the cover prices of $2.75 each—quite a bargain! I understand that accepting the books and gift places me under no obligation ever to buy any books. I can always return a shipment and cancel at any time. Even if I never buy another book from Silhouette, the 4 free books and the surprise gift are mine to keep forever.

215 BPA AJH5

Name	(PLEASE PRINT)	
Address	Apt. No.	
City	State	Zip

This offer is limited to one order per household and not valid to present Silhouette Romance™ subscribers.
*Terms and prices are subject to change without notice. Sales tax applicable in N.Y.

USROM-93R   ©1990 Harlequin Enterprises Limited

UNDER THE MISTLETOE

*Where's the best place to find love
this holiday season?* UNDER THE MISTLETOE,
*of course! In this special collection, some of
your favorite authors celebrate the joy of the
season and the thrill of romance.*

#976 DADDY'S ANGEL by Annette Broadrick
#977 ANNIE AND THE WISE MEN by Lindsay Longford
#978 THE LITTLEST MATCHMAKER by Carla Cassidy
#979 CHRISTMAS WISHES by Moyra Tarling
#980 A PRECIOUS GIFT by Jayne Addison
#981 ROMANTICS ANONYMOUS by Lauryn Chandler

Available in December from

ROMANCE™

SRXMAS

THIS SIDE OF HEAVEN

The miracle of love is waiting to be discovered in Duncan, Oklahoma! Arlene James takes you there in her trilogy, THIS SIDE OF HEAVEN. Look for Book Three in November:

A WIFE WORTH WAITING FOR

Bolton Charles was too close for comfort. Clarice Revere was certainly grateful for the friendship he shared with her son. And she couldn't deny the man was attractive. But Clarice wasn't ready to trade her newfound freedom for love. Not yet. Maybe never. Bolton's patience was as limitless as his love—but could any man wait forever?

Available in November,
only from

Silhouette
R O M A N C E™

SRAJ3

Share in the joy of a holiday romance with

1993 SILHOUETTE Christmas STORIES

Silhouette's eighth annual Christmas collection matches the joy of the holiday season with the magic of romance in four short stories by popular Silhouette authors:

**LISA JACKSON
EMILIE RICHARDS
JOAN HOHL
LUCY GORDON**

This November, come home for the holidays with

where passion lives.

SX93

He staked his claim...

HONOR BOUND

by
New York Times
Bestselling Author

previously published under the pseudonym Erin St. Claire

As Aislinn Andrews opened her mouth to scream, a hard
hand clamped over her face and she found herself face-
to-face with Lucas Greywolf, a lean, lethal-looking
Navajo and escaped convict who swore he wouldn't hurt
her— *if* she helped him.

Look for HONOR BOUND at your favorite
retail outlet this January.

Only from...

Silhouette

where passion lives.   SBHB

SILHOUETTE.... Where Passion Lives

Don't miss these Silhouette favorites by some of our most popular authors!
And now, you can receive a discount by ordering two or more titles!

Silhouette Desire®

#05751	THE MAN WITH THE MIDNIGHT EYES BJ James	$2.89	☐
#05763	THE COWBOY Cait London	$2.89	☐
#05774	TENNESSEE WALTZ Jackie Merritt	$2.89	☐
#05779	THE RANCHER AND THE RUNAWAY BRIDE Joan Johnston	$2.89	☐

Silhouette Intimate Moments®

#07417	WOLF AND THE ANGEL Kathleen Creighton	$3.29	☐
#07480	DIAMOND WILLOW Kathleen Eagle	$3.39	☐
#07486	MEMORIES OF LAURA Marilyn Pappano	$3.39	☐
#07493	QUINN EISLEY'S WAR Patricia Gardner Evans	$3.39	☐

Silhouette Shadows®

#27003	STRANGER IN THE MIST Lee Karr	$3.50	☐
#27007	FLASHBACK Terri Herrington	$3.50	☐
#27009	BREAK THE NIGHT Anne Stuart	$3.50	☐
#27012	DARK ENCHANTMENT Jane Toombs	$3.50	☐

Silhouette Special Edition®

#09754	THERE AND NOW Linda Lael Miller	$3.39	☐
#09770	FATHER: UNKNOWN Andrea Edwards	$3.39	☐
#09791	THE CAT THAT LIVED ON PARK AVENUE Tracy Sinclair	$3.39	☐
#09811	HE'S THE RICH BOY Lisa Jackson	$3.39	☐

Silhouette Romance®

#08893	LETTERS FROM HOME Toni Collins	$2.69	☐
#08915	NEW YEAR'S BABY Stella Bagwell	$2.69	☐
#08927	THE PURSUIT OF HAPPINESS Anne Peters	$2.69	☐
#08952	INSTANT FATHER Lucy Gordon	$2.75	☐

	AMOUNT	$
DEDUCT:	10% DISCOUNT FOR 2+ BOOKS	$
	POSTAGE & HANDLING	$
	($1.00 for one book, 50¢ for each additional)	
	APPLICABLE TAXES*	$
	TOTAL PAYABLE	$
	(check or money order—please do not send cash)	

To order, complete this form and send it, along with a check or money order for the total above, payable to Silhouette Books, to: *In the U.S.*: 3010 Walden Avenue, P.O. Box 9077, Buffalo, NY 14269-9077; *In Canada*: P.O. Box 636, Fort Erie, Ontario, L2A 5X3.

Name: _____

Address: _____ City: _____

State/Prov.: _____ Zip/Postal Code: _____

*New York residents remit applicable sales taxes.
Canadian residents remit applicable GST and provincial taxes.

SBACK-OD

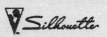